Also by Ouida Sebestyen:

WORDS BY HEART

Far from Home

A promise to keep, made to his mother before she died. A burden larger than himself. Now, with nothing left to do, to eat, to hope for, how will he hold this bare-bones family of his together?

As he set off for the Buckley Arms rooming house in the stillness of that dawn, he didn't see how God could love him and let him come to this. His fingers slid across the pocket of his overalls where the note was. Ten words that had the power to rearrange his life. The rickety child-letters his mother had formed wavered in two short lines, commanding him, "Go to Tom Buckley. He take you in. Love him."

Ouida Sebestyen has written a compelling and evocative story of a young boy's struggle to find the father who has never acknowledged him. To find a home. Overflowing with spirit and life, *Far from Home* enriches our understanding of the complexities of love and of what it means to be father and son. A book to touch all who read it.

OUIDA SEBESTYEN

Far from Home

An Atlantic Monthly Press Book
Little, Brown and Company
BOSTON   TORONTO

FIRST EDITION

Library of Congress Cataloging in Publication Data

Sebestyen, Ouida.
 Far from home.

 "An Atlantic Monthly Press book."
 SUMMARY: After the death of his mother, 13-year-old
Salty goes to take his place working for the Buckley
Arms Hotel where he begins to learn about the complexi-
ties of love and family.
 [1. Fathers and sons — Fiction] 1. Title.
PZ7.S444Far [Fic] 80–18328
ISBN 0–316–77932–6

ATLANTIC–LITTLE, BROWN BOOKS
ARE PUBLISHED BY
LITTLE, BROWN AND COMPANY
IN ASSOCIATION WITH
THE ATLANTIC MONTHLY PRESS

Designed by Melissa Clemence

BP

*Published simultaneously in Canada
by Little, Brown & Company (Canada) Limited*

PRINTED IN THE UNITED STATES OF AMERICA

To Corbin

Far from Home

CHAPTER ONE

WHEN the black ceiling he had stared at so long turned gray, and ready-or-not it was morning, Salty Yeager got up in the overalls he had slept in, and felt along the kitchen shelf for breakfast. A box had five crackers in it. Two and a half he gulped down. Two and a half he left on a tin plate for his great-grandmother, who was puffing out wide-spaced snores in the other room. He drank all the water he could hold, to fool his stomach into thinking he had fed it.

Outside, the sagebrush drooped with dew. He scrambled barefoot down a cold sand trail to the riverbank. At a sunken barrel that caught the seep from a slow spring, he dipped up a fresh bucket of water for Mam to use while he was gone.

As Salty crossed the yard again, a big gander let out a honk and came running on fly-swatter feet, rowing his bony wings. Salty squatted and stroked his white taffeta back, trying to shush him so Mam wouldn't wake. One blue eye and then the other glared at him with love. Suddenly the gander dipped into the bucket, swished the water happily, and took a drink.

"Quit that, Tollybosky," Salty whispered, grabbing at the gander's strong, snaky neck too late. Tollybosky nipped the top out of one of Mam's petunias blooming in a coffee can and let it drop. Salty yanked him back. "Behave yourself!

3

You can't do stuff like that from now on — you'll get yourself roasted for dinner."

The gander slapped at him with the hard hinge of his wing, but Salty held his neck at arm's length and met his one-eyed glare with a frown. The crazy old bird didn't know what he meant. Changes, worries, nothing like that meant anything. Maybe geese were lucky. He took the water into the kitchen, flicking out the white down that floated on it.

In the stillness, he gazed around in leave-taking. He would be back, but by that time he would know if they were going to take him. They had to take him. He could do what his momma did, and they took her. They had kept her fifteen years. So, goodby.

As he started out, a voice from the other room said, "Salty. Wear shoes."

He sighed and went to the door. His great-grandmother sat on the edge of her bed, coiling her white plait into a knob on the top of her head. The flab of her lifted arms wavered like something pale under water.

"How'd you know I was going?" he asked.

"I could tell last night you had decided." Her voice had the soft, slow strength of a root that could split rocks. "God love you, baby. I know it's me you're doing it for. I sure wish you didn't have to."

He didn't see how God could love him and let him come to this. He shrugged. "I wish I didn't neither, but I do. There's not nothing else left." To eat, he meant. To hope for. To try.

"Sell one of my oil wells," Mam said, hunting for her shoes with her slow bare feet. "My next-best diamond." She was joshing him. Maybe to show she was sorry to be denying him answers she couldn't give. "Some of these here silver dollars making lumps in my mattress." She smiled, forgetting that her teeth were already smiling at him from a glass of water on the

4

chair beside her bed. He tried to smile back, not sure she could see that far in the dimness, but the corners of his mouth began to wiggle the way they used to when he was young enough to cry.

"It'll be all right," he told her. Told himself, as he had over and over in the dark. "I'll just be doing what my momma did, won't I? It won't be no different, her living there and working for our keep or me doing it."

"It'll be different," Mam said.

"Maybe not. They must be nice. She was happy there. Her face was happy when she come home. Money come from there. Food. They must be nice." He trailed off, empty. Scared.

Mam leaned back on the two goose-down pillows she and great-grandpa had brought to Texas. Her smile crumpled. "Baby, don't fret yourself sick. Just go do what you have to."

His fingers slid across the pocket of his overall bib where the note was, crinkling gently like the beginning of a fire.

She said, "I wish to goodness I could be a help, instead of trouble. You ought not to be loaded down with burdens bigger than you are."

"I'm not," he assured her. "You took care of me, so I'm going to take care of you, that's all. I'm plenty big." He was, for thirteen, overgrown even, except for brains.

"I know you are," Mam's placid voice said. "You've made a fine, big boy. Your momma would of been proud of you. I am."

He waited. Finally he said, "Don't you have nothing else to tell me?"

"No, baby." Her hand fanned sadly, sending him off.

He left Tollybosky squawking at the gate and cut through the pasture sage. At the first cultivated field, he turned to follow the edge of ripe wheat hanging heavy in the June heat.

The field curved out like a giant claw, raking at the tar-paper house and the wild border of the river where he had spent his life.

He stopped and looked back. He knew he ought to plant his heels right there and say to God, You've taken enough. My momma and my home is enough. But his mind jumped like a phonograph needle into a worn groove: they had to take him, even if he lost the final thing he had to lose — his pride.

He walked between wheatfields for the first two miles. Then houses started. First the farm where he had mucked manure until they hired a real hand. Then others, two-storied and compact in the long sweeps of space because their builders had come to the top edge of Texas from places where the land was small. Families at breakfast glanced out as he passed swinging his shoes by their laces.

When he trudged over a rise, the Wickwire water tower was standing on its spider legs in the sun. The whistle at the oil mill blew. Its sound drilled sharply through the wall he had raised around his memories. He turned, expecting to see his momma beside him, smiling in her special silence as she lifted three fingers of each hand to tell him the time.

His breath began to come in puffs. His feet labored, scraping faster and faster until he was almost running. Beside him, beyond the spiked fence of Mount Zion cemetery, long tombstone shadows humped over the graves. They reached to draw him into their mystery, as they had drawn his momma. His eyes cut sharply to see. She was there but not there, as always, in the brier corner where the marble stones stopped and small tin markers staggered in rows. He halted in the road, panting, and looked directly at the place. *Don't grieve,* Mam had said to him the day they stood there in the February sleet. *She's with the Lord now. She can talk. And sing. And laugh. Be glad for her.*

6

He had tried. He had been glad for his momma. But for himself, he had grieved so hard in secret that he grew afraid he would bring muteness down again on her singing soul.

She used to let him walk to the edge of Wickwire with her, and there he watched as she marched into the heart of town and disappeared. There at the edge she always shook her head. When he was little, he used to think it was some kind of jail or hospital she went to, that let her out on Sundays to be with him. But Mam explained what she did, and why she stayed overnight in order to have breakfast ready early and to be on call if someone got sick in the night. Sometimes when things were slack she would come home on a weeknight. He would hear the car stop way down on the road in the dark, and he would fly through the sage to meet her coming along the wheatfield as the car lights disappeared. He would grab her hands, his joy darkened by the thought that early the next morning she would leave him again at the edge of town.

Of course, as he got older, he followed her in secret to the other side of Wickwire where she worked, stopping a block away to watch her go around toward the back door. But always, even when he went to school or ran errands or sneaked into the picture show, town had a sense of the forbidden about it. Even now, as he walked past the sign saying CITY LIMITS, POP. 6,003, SPEED LIMIT 10 MPH, WATCH FOR OUR CHILDREN, he felt his silent momma shake her head.

Yet it was her words on the note he carried, that had commanded him. Ten words had the power to rearrange his life.

All at once, trees lined the street, shading houses and watered grass. Wet roses and honeysuckle hung in a heaviness, as if the west and the south had suddenly overlapped on the edge of town. The strange, warm snow of cottonwood fuzz fell around him.

The water tower loomed up in an empty lot. Boys who

had graduated from high school in May had climbed up one night and printed SENIORS 1929 all over it with red paint. Not something he would ever do, he guessed. Graduate.

Houses gave way to stores. He detoured for proprietors sweeping the dust of their sidewalks into the wide, still streets. At the Pictorium, posters were still up for Tom Mix and His Wonder Horse Tony. He had almost got in to see that one, but the usher had been quicker than he was.

A new Model A, just out last year, stood in front of the Majestic Hotel. He ran his fingers over the shiny fender in the same respectful way he used to trace the words under the car-ad pictures in the magazines his mother brought from work. The hotel door opened and the smell of ham and coffee hit him like a fist in the stomach. A porter coming out to roll down the awning said, "Hey, you. Scram."

Salty lifted his hand as insolently as he dared and only let his elbow slide along the car. A boy about his age, coming out of the hotel with his father to get into that shiny thing and drive away, looked past him and yawned. Just as Salty yawned back in involuntary imitation, he heard the crunch of the porter's footsteps and whisked himself around the corner.

He had picked the street with the bakery. He stopped dead in his tracks and stuffed himself on the fragrance of warm bread. As he stared at the pies on their doilies in the window, he caught sight of his own reflected face, distorted into a long, big-mouthed funny-paper drawing under tan, mashed-grass hair. His cowlick pointed like a bird dog. He slapped it down. Move, he told the image. You're standing here because you don't ever want to get where you're going.

He sat on the running board of Feeney's bakery truck to put on his shoes and loped past the main part of town into the cheap fringe of little businesses and run-down homes. He knew what to look for: a big house, gray and two storied,

8

with a long double porch across the front, smothering in trumpet vines. But when he finally saw it, close, he felt a cool trickle of sweat across his ribs that was not from running.

It was shabby old, like a dignified bum who still thought he was somebody. He wished it looked prosperous and impressive. Because, this way, he hated to think that his momma had spent the last half of her life inside its walls.

Someone had already watered the lawn. Salty cut across wet grass, past a recently hand-lettered sign that said *Tourists Accepted.* Above the porch steps hung the other sign he had known he would see. Curly letters, too fancy, spelled out the grand and faded words. THE BUCKLEY ARMS. Why would the owners, he wondered, be ashamed to say plain Room and Board, or admit they ran a boardinghouse?

From somewhere a voice said in a whisper, "Could you do me a favor?" Salty froze, then jerked to find the sound. A man in his summer union suit was leaning over the banister of the upstairs porch, pointing down through the trumpet vine at the ground below. "I dropped my nose."

Salty's jaw slowly sagged. The man already had a pink sunburned nose, above a little-boy grin. He also had false rubber ears two sizes too large, and a red wig that had frozen in mid-explosion. His left arm, bent and bandaged, hung from a sling tied around his neck.

When he could tear his gaze away, Salty bent and parted the larkspur. Uncertainly he held up a celluloid nose attached to pretend spectacles.

"How about skinning up the beanstalk?" the man whispered. "I'd skin down, but —" He thumped his splinted arm.

Salty pulled himself up the crossbarred lattice until their hands touched. Instead of taking the nose, the young man caught Salty's wrist and guided him up over the banister. The prettiest woman Salty had ever seen up close was asleep on a

9

mattress on the porch floor. Her black hair rippled across the pillow, and the rest of her rippled under the coverlet, but her closed eyes left her face unfinished.

"Would you help me get this dumb thing on?" the man whispered. "It just came in the mail yesterday." He followed Salty's gaze. "She's going to wake up and find a very strange spiffy gentleman lying there beside her." He tried with his one good hand to hook the earpieces around his rubber ears. "Oh, incidentally, you don't need to mention to anybody that we move the mattress out here when it's too hot inside, do you?"

One of his ears fell off. Salty put it back on and adjusted the wig around it. They grinned at each other.

All at once a surge of hope set Salty's fingers tingling. He drew the note from his bib pocket and unfolded it. The rickety child-letters his momma had formed that last day in the hospital wavered in two short lines:

GO TO TOM BUCKLEY HE TAKE YOU IN
LOVE HIM

He held the paper out. The man read, and looked at him, and read again. His face flushed. He pushed the note back into Salty's hands, confused. "Look, I'm not who you want — this isn't for me."

"You're not Mr. Buckley?" Salty whispered, sagging.

"McCaslin," the man whispered back. "Hardy McCaslin." He couldn't seem to decide whether to smile or not in their shared embarrassment. "That beautiful lady asleep is my wife. My Rose Ann." They gazed down at her, struck shy. Her eyelids flickered, as though she were far away in her dream, in the past, or in darkness, hunting her way out of a place full of sound and dangers. "Well, now," he finally said, "we've got me straight. Who are you?"

"Salty. Yeager. Salty Yeager."

The spiffy gentleman held out his hand. Salty hesitated, then shook it. "It's Tom you want," Hardy McCaslin said, gesturing down again. "Around back." He helped Salty ease over the banister and started him down through the tangle of trumpet vine.

As his feet touched the ground, Salty heard Hardy Mc-Caslin's voice say without whispering, "Good morning, Madam. Is this bed taken?" The beautiful lady screamed. Then chuckles and protests and little private words drifted down on him like leaves as they lay hidden high up in the early sun.

CHAPTER TWO

Salty went around to the side of the house and leaned against the wall, wiping his sweating hands on his overall bib where the note creaked. Words began to play inside again. Just take me. That's all. Like me if you can. Be as nice as that guy up on the porch.

He went around to the back screen. Someone was coughing. In the kitchen, a fat woman fried potatoes at a big black stove. Behind her on a platter rose a pyramid of biscuits. His stomach squeezed up again. As he lifted his hand to knock, she saw him.

"Tom," she said.

A tall man in an undershirt came to the screen, with a razor in his hand and lather on his face. Suspenders hung down over his pants. "What is it?" he asked in irritation.

Salty's heart surged up and prepared him for running. The face he saw startled him worse than Hardy McCaslin's strange gentleman. Like the house, it was older than he expected, than he wanted it to be. He braced himself.

"Mr. Buckley? I'm Salty."

The lathered face looked down at him. In the long silence the woman came to stand beside her husband, wiping her hands.

"I'm Salty Yeager," he said to her. "I'm Dovie's boy."

"My stars," she said softly. "Dovie? Our Dovie?" She looked him up and down. "Tom, he's Dovie's boy."

Tom Buckley's face turned half away, clownish in its soap whiskers. "Your spuds are burning," he said.

She rushed back to the stove, light on her little gopher feet, and grabbed the skillet off.

"Well," Tom Buckley said. "What can we do for you?"

The woman was back. "Tom, I just can't believe it. Dovie had a boy. She never said — Well, of course she never *said!* But my goodness. Come in — Salty, is it?" Her face went properly respectful. "It was such a shock to us, too. Just so sad. I mean, all those years with us. We loved her like one of the family. And then so sudden like that."

"Yes ma'am," Salty said, letting her words run off him like rain off Tollybosky's back.

"We didn't know a thing about it till we got back from my niece's wedding, or we would have gone to the funeral and all. And after that, all through February Tom was doing his best to come down with pneumonia."

Tom cleared his rusty throat. "You're living with your grandmother, I take it."

"She's my great-grandmother," Salty said, feeling a flash of suspicion. Was he being tested? "Where we always lived."

Tom Buckley turned back to a mirror on the kitchen wall. Slowly he poised the razor and sliced a swath of lather from his long, taut jaw.

"That's over west of town somewhere?" The woman pointed vaguely south, not being the kind who felt directions instinctively. "Tom used to drive Dovie home sometimes in bad weather, but I —" She stopped and watched Tom shave.

"Out by the crossing," Tom told her. "Near where the old bridge used to be."

"That far? My. Not being able to *talk* to her, you know. There's so many things I just never . . ." She scooped a log-jam of golden potatoes into another platter. "I just never imagined what her life was like when she wasn't here."

Tom said, "Babe, honey, if you could slow down a minute we can ask him if there's something he needs."

"I need a job," Salty said. He had practiced saying it so many ways that it all came out in a gullywasher of words. "I want to come work for you like my momma did, take her place and live here, earn my keep — you wouldn't have to pay me. I can do everything she did, I did it at home while she worked here, I can cook beans and flapjacks, and wash clothes. I have to come. I asked for jobs but nobody took me. So I have to come."

Halfway through the flood Tom's razor stopped. Then it scraped deliberately up across the stubble of his neck. Salty examined their faces, hers staring directly, Tom's in the mirror, trying to see acceptance in their eyes.

"Not possible," the face in the mirror said.

His wife said, "Oh, Tom, now wait." Unconsciously she lifted her chin and tensed her cheek just as he did as he shaved. "Let's think about this. Since Dovie died — "

"No," he said.

"But Tom, since Dovie died we've needed somebody. All that work on the roof you've got to do. You know what the doctor said. And this boy here. I don't know. Couldn't we try it? For Dovie's sake?"

"No, we couldn't," Tom said. "No. We can't."

Salty said, "I didn't want to neither. Mam and me, we meant to manage, but we can't, is all, or I wouldn't never bothered you."

"Tom," the woman said. "Why not?"

14

For answer he wet a towel and put it to his face, pressing the last flicks of lather from the hard-set corners of his mouth. When he lowered it, Salty's heart sank. Tom's cold careful expression was not what he ached to see.

"We need more help around here," the woman said sharply. "Tom, it's summer and you still don't have your strength back. I can't do everything." He turned his stare on her. "I mean you try to do too much and over-exert . . ." Slowly the coldness of his gaze chilled her into silence. She went back to the stove and broke eight eggs into the skillet. She lifted two more. "Salty?"

He swallowed hard and said, "No ma'm. I ate at home."

"You don't understand," Tom said. "He means the great-grandmother, too. Living here. That's what he's asking."

She thought about it. "So?"

"So weigh it, Babe. Before you jump into this thing."

"I mean to work for Mam's keep, too," Salty said quickly. "I don't intend to be beholden to anybody. Specially you."

Tom smoothed his thin hair at the mirror. "You're a little short on manners, aren't you?"

Heat prickled Salty's face. Everything he tried to say came out backward. "I just meant because you was good to my momma."

Tom's eyes flicked to him. Then carefully, as if he had to practice making a speech, he said to the mirror, "Your mother was the best help we ever had. We miss her. We're sorry for all these changes. But we're not responsible for you, or an old lady we never saw, just because your mother scrubbed our floors."

"Tom!" the woman said. "My stars. That's uncalled-for."

"Are we?"

"Are we what? Responsible?" She looked bewildered. "What's that got to do with it?"

"Everything!" he said with razor sharpness. "Are we?" He spread his hands in anger. "Babe, what do you want?"

"Just, why don't we try it, that's all. We talked about who we could get to help, and then in he walks, like a sign from heaven. Dovie's boy —"

Without warning, Tom's big-knuckled hand swung out and rapped her across the cheek. She sat back against the stove and popped forward again, holding a hand to each injury.

"Oh, Lord," Tom said. Salty watched the hard edges of his mouth melt away until he was someone else. His different voice said, "Babe, you know I never did that before in my life. Babe. I don't know what happened." He tried to lock her in his arms, reaching around to comfort her scorched bottom, but she slanted away, still stunned. "Babe!" he begged. "Sweetheart, I'm just so tired. I didn't sleep last night, the tax notice came again yesterday and I couldn't — I just lay there, and now I'm taking it out on you." His hands fumbled to take hers and draw her back into the moment before he hit her. To Salty in the corner they seemed to be dancing to two different songs.

Babe pushed him away and began to cry. The fuzzy henna curls over her ears jiggled. She set the eggs off the heat and wiped her eyes with the potholder.

"Babe, please," Tom begged. He reached to touch her fat shoulders, the way Salty remembered his mother reaching out to wild things, animals in pain, offering her anxious, frightened love. "Babe, you mean the world to me."

"I know that," she said. "I know I do." With great dignity she let him touch her. "But, Tom . . ."

"But you want him. Is that it? You're determined? Nothing's going to persuade you different?"

"No, I don't if you don't, Tom. But it seems strange —"

"Now, wait." He drew his hands back. "It's not strange.

We don't know him." He turned to Salty. "Don't get the idea we'd be talking about anything permanent. It would be absolutely temporary. You understand? If we can't drum up some more business for this place, we're going to have to sell it."

Babe stopped crying in surprise.

"But there's some repair work, maybe two weeks' worth. Can you paint?"

Salty nodded. He would have said he could fly.

Tom sighed. "All right. Room and board. And you're going to have to sweat for it. Understand?"

"Yes," Salty said. The rehoned sharpness in Tom's voice stopped him from adding Sir, or even Thank you. Instead, he asked, "When can we come?"

Babe wiped her eyes, brightening a little. "Well, there's sure not a shortage of rooms. All we'll have permanent is the McCaslins, after the traveling people leave today."

"Can I start tomorrow?" Now that it was over, Salty suddenly needed to get out of the room, out of their presence, into fresh air. "I'll run tell Mam."

"Hold on." Tom caught him where the straps of his overalls forked, and hauled him back. "I'll take you in the car."

"You don't need to," Salty protested. It was the last thing he wanted. He needed to run till his breath whistled. He needed to yell words and strip the leaves off weeds.

"But Tom, breakfast —"

"I'm not hungry." Tom put on a work shirt hanging behind the door and settled his suspenders. He set his hat squarely on the line where his tanned forehead became white. Just as he reached the door, he hesitated and turned back to Babe. He laid two fingers to her cheek where the red mark was. "Are you all right?"

She leaned her head away.

CHAPTER THREE

THE car was an old Chevy with an Indian on the radiator cap. The garage had once been a shed; the wide doors were newer than the walls. Salty got into the front seat with Tom Buckley and mashed his cold hands between his knees. They backed out of the driveway.

Someone on the porch of the house across the street yelled to someone inside, "Take it out of the bathtub!" The words caught like cockleburs and hung in Salty's mind, mysterious, prickly. Take what? Why? It was like the words of his momma's note that had brought him burdened with questions to the man beside him.

Tom Buckley stared straight ahead. Salty supposed he had said everything, back in the kitchen. More than he had expected to.

They went through town. The new Model A was gone. They headed west along the dappled streets. The silence roared. Tom said to the Indian up ahead, "I was expecting you."

Salty crushed his hands together. His brain went hollow with surprise.

Tom said, "I don't like people barging in and rearranging my life."

"You run a boardinghouse," Salty said carefully. "New people come in all the time, don't they?"

Like a fighter jabbing suddenly to see what he was up against, Tom asked, "What do you want?"

"Just a place for Mam and me. To keep us together, the last two of us that's left." They were passing Mount Zion. Salty's head revolved, drawn by the shadows. "The man with the wheatfield come and said we couldn't live there no longer, it belonged to him now. Whoever owned it had sold it out from under us."

"You can cut out the razzmatazz," Tom said. "I owned it. I sold it. I needed money in a hurry, and it's all I had."

He stopped himself from saying, I bet. "You had your own house."

"The boardinghouse belongs to my wife and me together. This one didn't."

"What did you expect us to do?"

"I thought you had folks. I hoped you did. Off somewhere."

"Well, we don't. My grandma and grandpa died when everybody was having the flu."

"All right," Tom said. "I was wrong. So I'm trying to right it. You've got a place to live. Temporary. Remember."

"I'm remembering." He could taste bitterweed anger. "If I hadn't promised my momma I'd take care of Mam, I wouldn't come bothering you."

"Dovie wouldn't have asked anyone in the world to make that kind of stupid promise."

"It's not a stupid promise. Mam's not no trouble. But she's eighty-four. She fell down in the yard while I was at school and laid there all day till I got back." He stopped, softly blocking the moment when he had knelt and known their lives were tilting into a different balance, where he would be the strong one.

19

"So up you trotted to the Buckley Arms. Why?"

"Because my momma worked there fifteen years, is why. It was more like her home there than where I was, and you got to have more of her life than I did." He was surprised at himself. It wasn't the reason he had meant to give. But he plowed on. "So it was sort of like you owed me."

Salty watched the river arrive over the fields. Out there in those sandhills, he could kneel unerringly and peep into the nests of slick little rabbits or inch-long mice. He knew where the coons came down on baby feet. Out there he knew who he was and how he fitted in with everything else. But that was over. He took the note from his bib pocket and handed it to Tom.

Tom glanced at it. He put his hand back on the wheel, still holding the paper. It caught a draft and shivered like something living. "That's the main reason why," Salty said.

Tom slowed down, gazing far ahead at three crows sitting in the road as if he weren't sure how he was going to get past them.

"Why would she say that?" Salty asked.

"You've already answered yourself. If your mother didn't have any relatives, like you say, who else would she send you to?" Tom speeded up. "Look, if I wasn't so strapped for money right now I'd help you get settled in a more permanent place, with some kind of job."

"What about my daddy's folks?"

"What about your daddy's folks?"

"I never knew who he was." Salty drew a breath that couldn't seem to get to the bottom of his lungs. "Did you?"

"That's not really any of my business," Tom said. "That kind of thing. It could have been anybody."

"What do you mean?"

Tom shrugged. "Times were hard then. If she needed some extra money —"

"What do you mean, money? Hey, you be careful."

"I'm sorry," Tom said. He slowly crushed the note into a tiny paper marble and flicked it out the window. "Walking home by herself at night, something like that, is what I meant. Anybody who knew she couldn't talk." The crows at the last second leaped into the air and rowed away, as he drove the car over something small and dead in the road, intently making sure that no wheel touched it. "It's not something you're ever likely to know for sure."

"I'm going to know," Salty said stiff-mouthed. He watched the crows circle to drop again on their carrion meal. "When I had a momma it was different. But now, if I've got a daddy out there somewhere, I mean to know about it." He looked straight at Tom's profile against the bright window. "Why would she say that last part?"

"What last part?"

"Why would she say to love you?"

"Why not?" Tom said. "She was a loving person. She loved my wife; she and Babe, they were always — she loved everybody. You ought to know that. Her son ought to know that."

In his mind Salty felt the little white marble roll to a stop in the roadside grass. He had wanted to keep her note. Those were her final words to him, her last instructions. The voice he had never heard, saying goodby. She might have been trying to tell him everything she knew, everything he needed.

Yet as he watched Tom crush the paper up, he had felt the great weight of her request lift. It had just been two words. A suggestion.

"How come you threw away my note?" he asked.

A small, tight smile rearranged Tom's face. "I don't know

what your game is. Or what that great-grandmother may have put you up to. Maybe you started out just to get yourselves a place to stay by playing on our sympathy. But you listen to me — you're edging along something you're not old enough or smart enough to handle. Or even to know the implications of. But you understand me now: if you try to go a step further with it, I'll set the both of you out on the street in a second. You're not going to try this with my wife. She's had too many hurts in her life, she's not going to have any more. That's what I'm for. To see to it."

I could tell that when you hit her, Salty wanted to say, to scatter his gathering fear.

They stared ahead, wary of each other. In the heat, each dip of the road became a pool, a lie that emptied as they approached. He didn't know what Tom was talking about. Or maybe he did. Like seeing the mirage water, he wasn't sure.

"I'm not hard-boiled by nature," Tom said in a dropped voice. "I never raised my hand like that to her before. To anyone. Even in the war. I'm just telling you this, because —" He arranged the words with his lips. "Sometimes things happen —" He slowed, looking for the turnoff. "I was gassed. I didn't have much lungs left. Your mother added keeping me alive to all her other chores." They jolted off the highway pavement into ruts. Tom wiped one palm and then the other on his knees, taking fresh grips. "I'm sorry you think we took her away from you. I'm like Babe. I didn't really picture what it was like, out there."

They rode in under a cloud. Their eyes relaxed as the shadow ran before them down the ruts like a stroking hand.

Hesitantly Salty offered a part of himself, as Tom had. "I used to play like my daddy was in the war." He braced himself as Tom gunned off the road and made a path of his own along the edge of the wheatfield. "When I was little, I didn't know the war was already over and I played like he'd come back, you know, with all kinds of stuff, grenades and stuff he took off the Krauts."

"Germans," Tom said.

"Germans. And I thought he'd say, Look what all I brought you, because I was so little and stupid then I thought that's what he'd do. But when he didn't never come, I said, Well, he got killed."

Tom turned out across the trackless sage toward the house. "Killing people is what wars are for," he said, and got out in the yard.

Tollybosky sailed up and gave Tom a dig in the leg. Salty grabbed the gander and held his wings down while he paddled furiously under his arm. "He's as good as a watchdog," he said in apology.

"Better," Tom said rubbing his thigh. He looked at the tar-paper house the way Salty had, in a kind of leave-taking. A door in Salty's walled memory opened an instant. On darkness. Where? It shut again.

Mam came to the door. She had on her squashed black hat and funeral dress. Her cane was tied to her waist with shoe-string, and she propped herself on it like the picture of Columbus discovering America. Tom came to her and said, "Mrs. Yeager."

She had been crying. Her eyes were squinched small. "I'm ready," she told him. Her pose gave way and she looked back into the room. Salty could see two boxes on the table, tied, and a lumpy sack full of what must be their clothes. He was stunned. They were going *now*. She had known they would go. Before he did. She had packed while he was gone.

Tom stepped in and looked around. He said, "Would you

like for me to send somebody out to take what's left — the mattresses and so on? They might bring a few dollars."

"I'd be obliged," she said. "I'll miss my bed, but . . ." She started snaillike down the path. The front of her dress hung six inches lower than the back, sagging to fit her stoop.

"We'll fix you a nice bed, Mrs. Yeager," Tom said.

"Not the same," she said in her placid voice. "But it's too late to be choosy."

Tom looked at the river already shimmering itself hazy in the morning heat. "Did she — did she leave anything you'd like to take?"

"I have it," Mam said. She let Tom grasp her arm and help her into the front seat of the car. He went back for their things. As he put them into the car, a craziness grabbed Salty. He wanted to start his life running backward like picture-show film — Tom disappearing, winter there and the door opening on his momma home from work. He wanted it to stop there, frozen, hands raised, the steam from supper motionless. He calmed himself and with deliberation got into the back seat with Tollybosky.

"Now just a cockeyed minute," Tom said. He folded his arms.

"I can't *leave* him," Salty erupted. "He's tame. There's coyotes and hunters and kids with BB's. He's mine, I raised him. You don't have to do anything, I'll take care of him."

"But who'll take care of us?" Tom said.

Tollybosky settled heavily on Salty's knees and like a tiny, faraway trumpet breathed, "Whew."

"Look, now," Tom said wearily, "there's got to be another solution. Somebody who'll take him."

"But it's temporary," Salty reminded him. "He's all I got." He tried to smooth the scared jiggle out of his voice. "Please."

Tom looked from him to Mam and back. Tollybosky laid

a neat gray dropping on the car seat. "The same to you," Tom said. He slammed the back door shut and went to lock the house.

"I'm sorry, Mr. Buckley," Mam murmured after him. "We're a burden."

Tollybosky's sawtoothed bill reached for a ravel of upholstery, grating happily. Salty grabbed his neck. "We're not a burden," he told Mam. "He brought it on hisself — it was him that sold home out from under us."

"I know it was him," Mam said from the front seat. A little spiderweb hung from her hat. "But I'm going to tell you why he did it, and then I don't want you to ever mention it again to anybody. Who do you think let us live here rent-free all these years? Whose money do you think paid your momma's doctor bills and funeral?"

Tom came across the yard and got in. He started off with a jerk that flung Salty against the back of the seat. Tollybosky squawked, resettling, and they rode away through the scraping sage.

CHAPTER FOUR

"H E'S going to have to stay in the garage until we can fix up a pen," Tom said as they stopped in the driveway. "There's a crock in there you can put water in. Get the hose."

Salty did as he was told. Tollybosky strode beside him, shaking his feathers back into place after the ride.

"This won't be for long," Salty promised as he shut the gander up in the dark. He took the last box from the car and went in under the faded sign still lit by a white globe stained with brown shapes like continents.

In the hall, doors led off in all directions. His feet fell silent on a patterned rug that took off up the stairs. Mam couldn't have inched her way up there. He stumbled over a painted chalk bulldog squatting against the door to keep it from blowing shut. He managed to catch himself and the picture he dislodged when he hit the wall. It was a photograph of the Buckley Arms when it was new and white and proud, surrounded by broomstick trees and space. A little boy in knickers stood on the porch, new and proud too.

He could hear music coming from somewhere. He peeped into the parlor. The lid of a Victrola was propped up, and the McCaslins were dancing to a faraway orchestra captured on a record. They swayed without seeing him, looking different in clothes. Hardy McCaslin wore his own face and hair, too; a big improvement over the spiffy gentleman.

The record ended. Rose Ann McCaslin, tucked inside the bend of Hardy's broken arm, asked, "This is the way you'd like to spend your life, isn't it?"

He smiled against her hair and said, "Play 'My Isle of Golden Dreams.'" She put on another record and wound the handle up tight. As soft, sweet tropical music started, Hardy locked her again inside his stiff arm. He saw Salty and langorously winked.

Tom came out of a door beyond the stairs and said, "In here. Your Mam's all settled." Salty looked into a small, catty-cornered room with crawling wallpaper and a sunny window. Mam sat in a rocking chair. Her boxes were open on the bed, but the sack of clothes was gone.

"All settled," Mam agreed in her placid voice, but her white-knuckled hands seemed to be trying to steer the rocker down a river gorge.

Tom told him, "There's a little room next to this one."

"I want my momma's room," Salty said. "She had a room."

Tom stared briefly into Salty's set face. "Yes. She had a room." He went down the hall and opened one of the many doors. Salty followed him down a walled stairway into the basement. He had to know where she had spent all the years she hadn't spent with him. Little, high windows let in a grimy light. He could smell damp concrete and forgotten things. They passed shelves lined with jars of canned food tan with age, and Tom opened the door of a room. Salty could make out a bed, a low table, and a chair.

Tom pulled a string and a light bulb went on, rocking their shadows as it swung. Like the rest of the room, the narrow bed had been stripped. Salty put his hands on the chipped iron foot of the bed and looked at the gentle hollow in the mattress. When he finally turned around, Tom was gone.

Nothing else remained of his momma. The walls of concrete breathed a coolness. A faded makeshift curtain hung at the one window, but she had tied it back so she could see the stars. Then as he started out, he saw two brown felt slippers in the dark behind the door. He knelt and slid his hands into them, and slowly walked them up the wall until he stood with his forehead pressed against their dusty toes, swallowing back the tears.

How could she have been one of the family, like they said, down in that room?

When he went up the stairs again the kitchen was empty, but he could see Babe Buckley on the back porch, feeding lumps of clothes through the wringer of a jittery washing machine. It was time to earn his keep. He went out and began to catch the corners of cloth as they squeezed through, before they could wrap themselves around the gray rubber rollers. He recognized his clothes and Mam's. What did she think, that they had lice or something?

"Why, Salty!" Babe said, so brightly he knew she was remembering what he had witnessed that morning in the kitchen. "Thank you." She had a pearly, dimpled smile. "Dovie used to do that. We always used to do the wash together and talk." She laughed. "I talked, I mean, and she — answered. You know."

"Yes ma'm," Salty nodded, knowing how his momma's doubtful face slowly lit with understanding, like a field brightening behind cloud shadows.

"Well, so you're starting right off with a bang. All righty. You can hang these out while I get back to dinner, and then you can set the table and serve. After we eat and do the dishes we'll clean the rooms the tourists left last night and run another wash. You're a godsend, Salty — it's just too much for one person."

Or ten people, he thought, pinning the wash on the line.

Babe was frying chicken. Salty leaned against the doorframe while his head whirled. A rat in his stomach was gnawing its way out. Probably to attack the three rhubarb pies blushing on the table beside a perspiring pitcher of iced tea.

He rushed back and forth following her orders, clacking dishes together and jingling silverware in his trembly hands. From the dining room with its long, oilcloth-covered table he could hear her beating the potatoes, plop, plop, plop. She yelled through the door, "I expect your great-grandmother would like to eat in the kitchen with you."

Salty braked to a stop. "Yes ma'm. I guess." The idea hit him wrong. His being hired help had made Mam hired help too.

"Oh, foot, I'm going to call her Mam like you do," Babe said when he came back in. "And you might as well call us Babe and Tom like everybody else. You can say any name respectful." She dusted the cream gravy with pepper until Salty's saliva poured. "I had to call my papa 'Sir' till the day he died, but that didn't make me respect him. When you're little and wake up scared and want to yell 'Papa,' you just can't make yourself yell 'Sir.' "

She turned around to him, holding out a heaped plate. His rat did a flip-flop, and he put his hand out hesitantly. "I thought I was supposed to eat last."

"Oh, next time," Babe said. "I know when a boy's hungry."

He took the plate to the kitchen table and started at a polite pace. At the third bite he began to stab food faster, and in a minute he was cramming it in like a haybaler.

Babe murmured, "My stars," but nothing could stop him

from gobbling his way through one of the perfect moments of his life.

"It tastes like my momma's cooking," he said around a hot roll that he had squeezed into one bite.

Babe looked pleased. "We taught each other." She spooned more green beans and cole slaw into the empty spaces on his plate. "We worked good together, Dovie and me. I just miss her so bad." She went quickly into the dining room and rang a hand bell.

Tom came in from outside and washed his hands at the kitchen sink. As he moved on into the dining room, Salty piled a plate for Mam with wishbones and gravy, gripped by the sudden fear that it would all be taken away and eaten before he could provide for her. He shot down the hall and brought her back to the kitchen. He set her down before the bountiful mountain.

Mam said, "I know the Lord provides, but He didn't have to provide it all in one meal."

"Eat," Salty hissed joyfully, and rushed to take in the last two platters. Hardy and Rose Ann were sitting down.

"This is Dovie's boy," Babe said. "This is Salty."

"Is that a fact?" Hardy stood up, grinning in friendly conspiracy, and took the heavy platters from him, one by one, in his good hand. "I'm Babe's nephew. The family sponger." He remembered his manners and sobered. "We've been here since December — we knew your mother. We're sorry she died."

"Hardy!" Rose Ann pressed her napkin to her lips and said behind it, "Don't blurt things out like that."

"Why not? I'm sorry she died."

"I am too," Salty agreed, relieved to be able to say it. He went back for the pitcher of tea.

"I'll pour that for you," Hardy said, taking it. Salty carried around the goblets Hardy filled, and stood back waiting for instructions.

Tom said to him, "I got a roll of chicken wire put up for that web-footed watchdog of yours."

"He'll be glad," Salty said, holding back Thank you with a bleakness that matched the basement room where he would stay. They had just reminded him again that he wasn't Dovie's boy. He had been. Now he wasn't anything.

"Is a goose what I've been hearing?" Hardy asked. "I thought maybe the Eversoles across the street had another kid."

Everyone laughed except Rose Ann and Salty, whose mind automatically recalled: *Take it out of the bathtub. . . .*

Babe leaned to Rose Ann. "Sugar, you're not eating. Has the heat got your appetite?" She drank deeply from her goblet and suddenly cracked it sloshing to the table. "Oh, my *stars*," she screamed, scraping back her chair. "Tom! In my glass!"

Hardy exploded with laughter. Salty stood transfixed as Tom lowered a spoon through the ice of Babe's goblet and lifted up a cockroach. Babe screamed again and batted it away, while Hardy fell into his plate, cackling with delight.

In the middle of her third screech, Babe's horror changed to disbelief. Her eyes riveted on Hardy. "You bamboozler," she yelled. She poked the cockroach. It fell out of the spoon upside down and lay perfectly still. "It's not real. Of course it's not real, you slick-fingered joker. There's never been a cockroach in this house!"

Now Tom was laughing too and patting her arm. "He took you again. You're never going to learn." She rocked a minute, fighting embarrassment, then threw back her head and laughed with him, admitting it.

Rose Ann tugged at Hardy's sleeve, not laughing. "Honestly, Hardy. Not a day goes by that I don't swear I'm married to a little boy."

"Just so you notice I'm a big boy while the nights go by," Hardy chuckled. He had laughed till he cried. He pulled out a neat handkerchief and blew his nose. An instant before it happened, Salty guessed — the handkerchief was a trick too. A fierce trumpet blast erupted from it, flattening all of them back into their chairs. Salty doubled up with a shriek of pure joy.

"Oh, Hardy, that is vulgar!" Rose Ann's pale skin went pink. "When are you going to grow up?" She turned to the others. "I apologize."

The laughter slid out of Hardy's face, leaving a small fixed smile like something stuck in the bottom of a cup.

"Give him time," Tom said.

Babe giggled. "Oh, better yet — have a baby, sugar. You'd be surprised how fast he'll change into a real, steady, bringing-home-the-bacon father."

"You'd be surprised how fast I'd send it right back where it came from." Hardy wrapped the artificial cockroach clumsily in his trick handkerchief and put them in his pocket.

Rose Ann said, "Excuse me. I have letters to write." She went out. No one spoke. Salty picked up her napkin and laid it on the table.

"Did I say something wrong?" Babe whispered.

Hardy shook his head. "She's — I don't know — preoccupied about something. Nothing anybody says hits her right." He laughed. "Especially advice to have a baby, when we're trying our double damnedest not to."

Tom said, "Seemed like things were going better between you two lately."

"Oh, we have a lot of good moments," Hardy said. "Between a lot of bad hours."

Mam had gone when Salty carried the dishes back to the kitchen. Her plate was empty except for two wishbones she had left for him to pull. Hardy came in and held one out to him.

He didn't know what to wish. To stay in the Buckley Arms for good? To know who he was, to know what more he was than Dovie's boy? He couldn't risk leaving wishes that big to chance. He looked at Hardy's strained face, and just as they braced their wrists to snap the little forked bone, he said, "Let's don't."

CHAPTER FIVE

SALTY grabbed a spoon he was about to pour out with the sludge of his dishwater. Breakfast and dinner dishes were done, but the heaviness he felt was more than tiredness and too much food. This was the way it was going to be. People. Work. New ways and new problems that he never had at the river. His feet steamed in his shoes. He would have to find a bathroom soon, instead of stepping out behind the house. And Tollybosky was going to be trouble — he could feel it.

He could see the temporary fence Tom had strung up at the back of the garden. It had a peach tree for shade, but only bits of grass. He would have to ask permission to let Tolly forage on the lawn or along the alley where the weeds grew. And he would have to scrabble in the garbage for the cabbage leaves and bits of vegetables Babe threw away.

As he watched, Tom opened the garage door and let Tolly out. Tolly charged him again, head down, neck stretched, hissing like a locomotive. Tom tucked him, biting and scratching, into the makeshift pen. While Tom rubbed a cut on his hand, Tolly angrily twitched all his feathers back into smoothness and let out a great honk of triumph.

"Your clothes are dry," Babe said at the kitchen door. She

was holding out Salty's other pair of overalls. "If you've finished, you can get your bath and change."

He nearly dropped the dishpan. It was going to be worse than he had imagined. He wiped and tidied as long as he could, but she stood holding his clothes, as determined as he was. Finally he hung his cup towel up and followed her to one of the doors in the hall.

She handed him his overalls and shirt. "I noticed there wasn't any underwear with your things. I'll bring you some of Tom's."

He went in and shut the door to a crack. "No ma'm. I don't need none."

"You will wear underwear," she said evenly.

"Not his, I won't." He sat on the edge of the tub, not sure how far he dared cross her in something so personal.

Babe's footsteps went away. He waited, apprehensive, wondering how he could be angry at someone who cooked such good food. She returned and said, "I'll hang them here on the knob. Then I'll tell your great-grandmother not to unpack until we agree on some rules around here."

He could imagine her pearly smile growing edges of broken seashell as she waited. Under all that fat softness, she was a sack of cement. He opened the door and took the old-fashioned cotton drawers from the knob.

Babe looked earnest. "Salty —" she began, but he closed her off and ran the water until she went away.

He had never taken a bath in a real bathtub before. He didn't know how full he was supposed to fill it, but an inch seemed like plenty. As he dried, he could see from the window the plants he already knew from the cuttings his momma had brought home over the years and coaxed to grow in the sandhill wind. He could hear children screaming in the house across the street. He was not used to children. He went to school when they made him, and saw kids there, but he could do without them. He liked the river better, by himself.

His shirt and overalls were so clean they crackled. The double-stitched denim chaffed like saw grass, but he could stand it till they mellowed out in a few days. He squeezed Tom's underwear into a nearly empty box of Epsom salts in the back of the bathroom closet.

Out in the hall he poked around a little bit, touching things. Lacy curtains. Plush wallpaper. With only a few squeaks he eased up the stairs, but the McCaslins had closed their door.

When he sneaked back down, Mam was sitting in her chair in her stocking feet, looking weary. Everything was unpacked, and the room looked neat. "You all right?" he asked.

She patted his clean overalls admiringly. "Better off than I deserve to be, I expect."

"You need anything?"

She tapped the bulge in her pocket where she kept her can of snuff. "I could sure use a spit can if you find one."

"I'll try," he promised, wondering what Babe would think. Her ideas on snuff-dipping were bound to be as firm as her ideas on underwear. Back in the kitchen she was already jangling supper pans. He sighed, and went to help.

He expected to see tourists at supper with everyone else when he carried the soup into the dining room, but nobody had stopped for the night. Only Babe and Tom and Hardy were at the table. Babe was saying in a low voice, "How about your cousin, couldn't he use some help in the store?"

"The boy, maybe," Tom said. "But not if she's part of the parcel. If we do sell, they'll just —" He saw Salty and his voice changed tone. "Why don't you pull us some fresh onions to go with these butterbeans?"

They had been talking about him and Mam. He could tell by their faces. They were already planning how to pass them along to somebody else. Salty yanked onions from the garden as fast as he could, but by the time he got back with them, Tom and Hardy were eating in silence, and Babe was carefully slicing pie.

While Salty did the dishes again, Babe put out another washing to dry overnight. She took off her rings and kneaded dough for next day's rolls. He put dried fruit to soak for breakfast. They cleaned up again. She smiled at his tired face. "You did fine today, Salty. Go outside now and cool off a few minutes while I make up your bed. Then you better fall in — we get up at five."

He went out and found a couple of cans in the garbage barrel to take to Mam. She was sitting on the edge of the bed in her nightgown, just the way she had sat long ago and in a different world that morning.

"Look at you," she said lovingly, taking his hand. "Clean clothes. We're eating high off the hog, baby. Electric lights. Running water." He smiled, glad for her. "They're decent folks, Salty. To give us a roof over our heads and let us stay a family. Don't forget it."

He nodded. It would only hurt her to know how much more he needed than food and shelter, how hungry he was for more love than she could give him. "Don't get used to this," he warned her. "They're not going to let us stay. Even if they don't sell this place."

She drew him close. His overalls crinkled in her rootlike grasp. "We're here now."

He went down the hall. A radio was squeaking music. He saw Tom reading under a fringed lamp in the parlor. Not exactly reading, but staring into the gray wall of his paper.

The light over the front door still burned hopefully. Moths

spun like uncertain planets around it. Salty sat on the steps and took off his shoes.

Children — the ones who lived across the street, he guessed — were shouting in the dark. He watched their indistinct forms bob back and forth, blinking words and squeals like fireflies: You're *it!* Nuts! No *fair!*

He eased out to the sidewalk under the tree shadows. Someone on a creaking bicycle went up and down, singing "Yes, We Have No Bananas." They all sounded so safe. In the dark tonight, they would know where the bathroom was and what they would see out their windows in the morning when they opened their eyes.

The bicycle stopped in front of him in the street. A girl-voice said, "Who's over there?"

He was not sure she meant him. He gazed silently at the sturdy gray blob of her dress.

"You a tourist?" she asked. Some of the others stopped shouting and came closer. "Where you from?"

"I live here," he said as boldly as he could.

"Bunk! You don't neither." She let the bicycle drop on its side and came close to stare at him. She had a round face below what might be gingery hair in daylight, and she was shaped like a pickle jar.

Someone at the edge of the group said, "I'll see you, Idalee," and drifted off down the street.

"Okay," she yelled, and turned back to Salty. "What's been making that screechy noise all day over here?"

"I brought my gander."

"What's that? Can we see it?"

"Not tonight." He pulled himself taller, pleased that Tolly had attracted their attention.

"Says who?"

"Me."

She picked up her bicycle and gave the bell a ding. "So what? I've seen ducks before."

"Ducks! He's a goose, a white Embden goose. He's taller than that little kid yonder."

"You calling my little sister a goose?"

He sighed and didn't say, You know her better than I do. The light went on in the narrow basement window. Babe was making up his bed.

The girl said, "Is that your room? That's where the loony-bird stayed, when she worked here."

He froze at the undreamed-of words, his mouth fixed in astonishment. He had to say something to defend his momma, but his jaw locked.

"She was scary," she announced. "When we first moved here she tried to put curses on everybody."

"You're a liar!" He clamped his teeth over all the words he knew to describe her, cast one glance for watchers, and shoved her off her bicycle hard enough to crack the sidewalk.

She made a mill-whistle scream and leaped up, too well-padded and angry to be hurt. "You're in trouble," she bellowed. "You're going to get it when I tell my daddy. He'll turn you inside out."

Salty's stomach began to flop helplessly, the way it did in his nightmares. His feet begged to carry him away and hide him till he could wake up, but he dug his toes into the grass.

Tom came to the front door. "You kids break it up out there." He reached inside to a light switch, and the little glowing world above the door went black. As if he had been switched off too, Salty tore across the lawn and around the side of the house. His heart pounded. All he could think of was grabbing Tolly from his pen and taking off for the river, his unquestioning river, his home. But he forced himself calm. There was no place to run to anymore. No one to run to.

The snotty girl was still yelling, but farther away, from the safety of her own front porch. He guessed he was in bad trouble. He guessed her father and Tom and the whole rest of the world would land on him now.

The little white ghost marched up and down behind the wire. He went in and sat in the deepest shadow. Nobody called him. No one came looking. Tolly stood by his side, clicking like a sewing-machine as he tried to make a meal of Salty's toes.

Mosquito bullets whined past Salty's ears. He squeezed himself tight over his knees and let them draw blood. The lights went out across the street. Then upstairs. He guessed he was safe. Darkness began to release its own sounds: tree whispers, voices calling. A distant piano played something sad. It made him feel lost. Misplaced. Like the fireflies asking, Here? Here? He was glad geese lived a long, long time, as long as people.

When Tolly settled and tucked his head, Salty got up. He was stiff. It wouldn't have surprised him if they had locked him out, but they hadn't. He felt along the hall, trying to recall the way to the basement. Finally at an open door he could smell the dampness of cement and see the faint glow of the light Babe had left on for him. He tiptoed down the stairs and went into his momma's room. A pair of green pajamas hung at the foot of the freshly made bed. He slung them into the corner and yanked out the light. The sheet was as cool as dew to his chafed and bitten skin. He wondered if his momma knew he was there. All at once he felt so scrawny and exposed that he pulled the top sheet up and curled small into the hollow she had left him.

The house ticked and settled over his head, as heavy as a mountain. A trapped moth tapped like fingers on the glass. Please. I want to get out of this place.

He dreamed Hardy was blowing his trumpet handkerchief.

He jerked awake in the dark. It was Tollybosky, squawking loud enough to jar the whole neighborhood out of bed.

Salty grabbed his overalls, but got both feet started down the same pants leg. He hopped and stumbled until he got it right, and sprinted up the stairs.

At the pen, he knelt and waited for the white blur. "Listen, you've got to keep quiet," he warned it. "It's the middle of the night. You've just *got* to." It wasn't going to work, otherwise. He could feel trouble hanging like a hawk over them, ready to strike. But how could Tolly, so glad to see him, know that?

When he started up the back steps he took an extra one that wasn't there, lurched forward, and knocked the garbage can off the porch. He leaped after it, gritting his teeth to stop the clatter of tin cans and bottles as they rolled everywhere. Furiously he gathered them up, grabbing at moon shadows on the sidewalk by mistake. Tolly was telling the world he had caught a burglar. Salty scooped up everything that didn't run through his fingers, and set the can back on the porch. Back home he could have walked a mile at night without making a sound. He felt stupid.

The jogs and turns that were supposed to take him to the basement seemed to be backward. Unexpectedly he was at a closed door. He thought he heard Mam gasping softly behind it, and opened it to see what she needed. Springs jounced and a lamp went on. Tom was sitting up in a ruffled pink bed beside Babe, looking like a frog on a doily.

"Good Lord," he said tiredly. "What is it?"

Babe rose up in a sheen of cold cream. She and Salty gaped in mutual astonishment.

"Don't you know how to knock, damn it?" Tom hissed. He seemed to be seeing for the first time, with Salty, the fluffy room full of Jesus pictures and the lamp shaped like a morning glory that flared down on his spiked hair. "Get the hell out of here." He pulled the lamp's chain, and Salty bolted in the dark, sideswiping the door frame with a thud.

The black hall took off in the wrong direction toward a slit of gray. He groped toward it and saw that it was the open front door. A moment too late he remembered the chalk bulldog on the floor. His toes smashed against it. He hopped out onto the porch and pressed his burning face against the cool leaves of the trumpet vine. He was hopeless. He wasn't going to live to find his bed.

When a hand touched him, he jumped a foot on his bruised toes. Hardy's voice said, "Oh, sorry. I thought you saw me." He was sitting on the top step in the vine's shadow. "What's your trouble?"

"Nothing," Salty blurted. "I was hot so I come out. What's wrong with that?"

"Not a thing," Hardy said. His voice had darkened with the night.

Salty hesitated, glad to have his lie accepted, but held most by the changed voice. "I can't keep Tolly quiet."

"Give him a few days to get used to things."

"But if he keeps everybody awake . . ." He needed more assurance. "They'll boot me and him both out on our ears. And Mam."

Hardy held out his good hand. "Sit."

Salty stared at him without moving. Hardy seemed different without a lot of people to bounce off of, but it was hard to tell when he was acting: the times he was happy-go-lucky, or now, when he seemed sad.

Hardy asked, "How come Tom is taking you all in like this? You related?"

"What do you mean? No. We're not. My momma worked —"

"I know all that," Hardy said. "I just wondered." He dropped his outstretched hand. The note he had read by mistake that morning reduced them to silence.

He knows I hoped he was Tom, Salty thought. He knows I wanted him to be the man my momma sent me to love.

"I liked your mother," Hardy said. "That marvelous listening stillness about her. Those medieval hands and feet. Long, like yours. I wish I could have painted her picture."

"Are you some kind of artist?"

"I tried to be, among other things. Artist, actor, poet. Hero." Hardy clawed at his broken arm. "Damn, I stink. Did she ever talk — I mean, was she born that way?"

"I don't know," Salty said. He knew. Mam said when his momma was little her daddy had locked her in a trunk, and when he let her out next day she was that way; but why should he tell a stranger? Maybe she could have talked, after that, if there had been anything powerful enough to say.

A fancy car went slowly past, open topped, its wire spokes twinkling. "Stutz Torpedo," Hardy mused. "Slumming in Wickwire. Probably bootlegging himself into a millionaire. Swanky clothes. Jazz babies falling all over him. While I sit here stinking."

"It could be me," Salty said. "I knocked over the garbage can."

He heard Hardy's grumpy chuckle. "Well, then, we'll stink together. Through thick and thin. Spick and spin." He stood up and slid a hip flask into his pocket. "Sick and sin? I get the feeling it's past my bedtime. Yours too."

At his touch, Salty's throat squeezed so tight it brought tears to his eyes. "Can't find it," he whispered.

"Can't what?"

"Find the basement." He began to grab leaves as fast as he

could with his shaky fingers. "I don't know where things are. I want to go home."

Hardy came a step closer. "Well, home's here, now," he said in his daytime voice. He opened the screen. "Come on." He guided Salty down the black tunnel of the hall and stopped at a door. "Bathroom. Righto?" He went on. "Two more doors, then the basement." He went down the stairs, sliding his good hand along the rail. Everything fell into the right position all at once, and Salty moved ahead into the room, waving his arm until he hit the light string.

"Mercy-mercy," Hardy said softly, looking around. "It's not exactly the Ritz."

"It's all right." Salty sat firmly on the bed and gripped the mattress edge with both hands. Nobody, not even Hardy, was going to tuck him in.

"It's not all right." In the light, Hardy's face matched his tired, subdued voice. "But it doesn't get much better as you climb the stairs." He tried to strike a smile in Salty from one of his own, but nothing came. His face sagged again. "Not scared or anything, are you?"

Salty lifted his mosquito-bitten shoulders in a shrug of uncertainty.

"Happens to all of us," Hardy said. His toe poked the pajamas crumpled on the floor. "I see you and Babe are hitting it off fine. Remember what she said at dinner that made Rose Ann walk out? Well, good old Aunt Babe had guessed it. Even before I did."

"Guessed what?"

"About us. Rose Ann dropped the news on me this afternoon — boom." He took the cockroach out of his pocket and let it fall on the pajamas. "You think you've got a raw deal? I need a job and two hands and last month's rent money, and what do I get instead? The biggest little accident that can happen."

"What's that mean?"

"It means I've got to turn myself into a bringing-home-the-bacon daddy before Christmas." He pulled the light string. His footsteps moved toward the door. "Looks like you and I have our troubles coming. Want to stick it out together, through kick and kin?"

Salty didn't say anything. He listened until Hardy's steps faded into the rug at the top of the basement stairs. Then he got up and found the cockroach and put it under his pillow, just in case he should want to touch it in the night.

CHAPTER SIX

Mam came in next morning and tried to fry the sausage. Salty knew it wasn't going to work, the minute Mam and Babe collided at the stove and a raw egg flew into the oatmeal.

"Get her and that cane out of here before I break my neck," Babe ordered under her breath. She had her cement look again. "You better talk plain to her, Salty. Or I will."

Mam was covering the platter of eggs with a cup towel the way she did back home to keep flies off of things. He coaxed her out into the backyard to look at Babe's garden. "She's just lonesome, is all," he told Babe cautiously. "She's not used to sitting in a room all by herself. She's used to cooking."

"Well, I can't help that," Babe said. "Can I?" Her eyes glanced away, as cautious as his.

He didn't know what to do. He looked out at Mam and went back into the dining room where they were waiting. Tom was pouring coffee. He looked grumpy, as though he'd lain awake all night under his morning glory.

Hardy looked tired, too, but he gave Salty a quick grin and said, "Mercy, aren't we a bunch of flat tires this morning." He had slipped a make-believe gold tooth over one of his own, but no one looked up to see it flashing. "I got a great hash-house joke for you, Babe." Babe gulped her coffee with a taking-medicine face. "Rube joke?" he asked around. "Drummer joke, peachy, snappy, or red-hot joke?"

Tom stabbed two fried eggs from the platter. "I've got a joke for you. It looks like it's going to rain on that sieve we've got for a roof. And the bill for the septic tank's due."

"Tom, not while we're eating," Babe said.

Hardy reached into his pocket. He leaned across the corner of the table and pinned a celluloid disk to Tom's shirt pocket. It said *Ain't It Hell to Be Poor?*

Babe laughed in spite of herself. "Where do you get those goofy things?"

"He has a whole catalogue," Rose Ann answered for him. "He orders tons of stuff. Tons."

"I thought he was broke," Tom said. "Too broke to pay rent."

Hardy looked around at the faces. "What is this? You know some money's coming." He lifted his broken arm.

"How'd you break it?" Salty asked, forgetting himself.

"I fell off a church." Hardy tried to stuff the grubby cotton back under the splint so he could scratch. "I was painting the steeple and launched myself right off the roof. Tried to land on a deacon, but he sidestepped me. Maybe God was trying to tell me something."

Salty swallowed his giggle when no one else laughed. What did they see wrong about Hardy spending the last of his money on tricks and jokes? People needed to laugh and forget their troubles just as much as they needed food. "You can still do a lot of things with a broken arm," he said helpfully. He suddenly remembered about the baby coming, and got red. So did Rose Ann.

Hardy fished another button from his pocket and slapped

it on Salty's overall bib. It said *Sign Off, Kid*. But his fake tooth gleamed as he grinned, understanding.

While Salty was cleaning up, Mam peeped in from the porch. When she saw he was alone she came in and took the soapy dishrag from him. "Maybe you better not, Mam," he said.

She began to swipe plates, leaving bits of stubborn but well-washed egg here and there. "I want to. I'm not just a dead weight around here. There's things I can do. Go feed Tolly and let me work."

He stood beside her, wanting to say, When you're eighty-four, people are supposed to do for *you*. But he set out the breakfast he had saved back, and left. For a minute he gazed up at the roof. He had patched the roof a lot of times at home. With a ladder he could get up there and look it over.

The sprinkler was going in the side yard. Salty led Tolly under it and let him pluck the wet grass. Babe started around from the front porch, but backtracked quickly as Tolly snaked his neck and rushed at her. "Get that thing away from me," she yelled from the safety of the porch. "I'm out of wax and Tom's gone. You'll have to run and get some." She held up a can. "Like this, and here's the money on the rail." She and Tolly glared at each other. "Shoo!" Tolly shook off a spray of water drops and felled a tall lily with one bite before Salty could grab the money and rush him back to his pen.

The nearest hardware was across the tracks in a dilapidated end of town, downwind from the rendering plant. He saw a Help Wanted sign at the ice dock as he passed, but there wasn't a chance they'd hire *him* to hoist hundred-pound blocks of ice into people's cars.

He spotted a baseball in a fence corner and went along bouncing it off walls until it caromed from a wooden awning and hit the back of a woman walking slowly ahead of him.

He ducked his head between his shoulders. The woman stopped in the middle of the sidewalk, jerking her head back and forth. The ball rolled into the silent street. She looked at it and then at Salty. To his dismay she raised her hands to her face and began to cry.

He gathered himself to run, then ungathered. She had suddenly lurched toward a burned-out café with a broken front window. He watched in amazement as she eased down on the brick window ledge, her hands pressing the charred wood and shards of glass that had fallen on it.

"Didn't mean to hit you," he blurted from a safe distance.

She looked dazed. When she wiped her tears, her blackened hand left a streak under one eye. "You didn't hurt me," she said. "I just — it startled me."

She had a husky voice. Her short hair and freckles would have made her look like a boy, but her middle ballooned out the way Rose Ann's would by December. It looked as if she had walked the streets all night, but he didn't think girls like that had babies much.

She asked, "How far am I from some kind of hotel?"

He lifted his shoulders to say he was not sure. All he knew was that he should be getting Babe's wax, but the despair in her eyes stopped him.

"Could you show me how to get to one?" She pushed herself heavily to her feet. "I think I've got to lie down somewhere." She stopped and looked at him, to see whom she was telling all this to. Her eyes had dark circles, even the one without the soot smudge. She glanced around as a car passed on the quiet street, and abruptly let out a rush of air that could have been a tiny laugh or a sound of grief.

"I'm kind of in a hurry," Salty said awkwardly. "Maybe if I told you how to get to the main part of town —"

She suddenly looked so tired he was afraid she would fall.

He wondered if he should take her arm before she toppled over and made a pancake out of her baby.

"You hungry?" he asked. "When did you eat last?"

She studied him again. "Yesterday, at noon. Later, after I'd bought the ticket, I realized I didn't have any money left."

She wasn't making sense, but Salty gunned his courage. "I work at a boardinghouse. I can get you some stuff to eat, a lot closer than a hotel. Free," he added, glancing at the purse she said was empty.

"You must work for nice people." She watched a draft inside the gutted building catch up gray ash and whip it against the black humps of unrecognizable things. Abruptly she started off beside him, balancing her load uncertainly, spraddle legged.

He guessed he had overstepped himself again. But he might as well catch it for everything at once — for Tolly and for pushing the snotty girl and bursting in on Tom and Babe and bringing in a stranger to eat free. "You live around here?" he asked her.

He had gone a few yards before he noticed she wasn't following. He came back to her. Distress had glazed her face. "Kansas City," she said.

He couldn't figure her out, but he waited, glancing as she did at the next car that passed. They had gone another block when she swerved off catty-cornered across the street. "Hey, lady!" He caught up. She was making those gasps that he saw now were sounds of pain. "Lady?" She went faster, almost tripping at a curb.

"I can't go with you. With no money. I couldn't —" She swiped her face again, leaving more soot streaks.

"But, lady, listen. Stop a minute. Where can you go?"

She slowed down. Her hands were shaking like her breath, but her chin came up sharp and determined. "I don't know."

"Well, eat and then decide," he coaxed. She hesitated. Something inside her rounded belly gave a knock. It really moved. Salty blinked. He had never seen that happen. Before he thought, he said, "My friend's going to have a baby, too."

She placed her hand on the spot that had bounced. "Is she?"

"No. He is. I mean — *they* are, but he's my friend." He saw something else. She had a wedding ring. He said carefully, "Is there anybody I can go find to help you? Your husband or anybody?"

She covered that hand with the other one. Her face went white under the soot smudges. "Can I hold to your arm?" She reached out to him. "Do you know a shortcut?"

He caught her elbow and guided her as fast as he could into an alley. It would lead them into the street the Buckley Arms was on, five blocks away. Her hand hauled on him like a grappling hook.

She was really nutty. From what she'd said, she'd spent all her money to get to Wickwire, and now she didn't know why she'd come.

"You can make it," he assured her as her steps slowed.

"Trying," she whispered. "So hot. Is it far?" Without waiting to know, she folded her knees and dropped to the ground between two rattling garbage cans.

Tom and Hardy carried her to the upstairs room, one on each side, the way they had eased her into Tom's car when they got to the alley. She had been trying to get to her feet when Salty leaped from the back seat, yelling, "Wait — it's us!"

Babe came out of the room with a tray of empty dishes and closed the door. They waited at the foot of the stairs. "Asleep," she told them.

Salty felt their eyes converge on him. He had already told them all she had told him. "I guess she feels safe now."

"This is all we need," Tom said. "Getting messed up in somebody's family problems. I still think we ought to call in the sheriff."

"But if she hasn't done nothing —"

"She's done one thing, it looks like. Run away from her husband. He's got a right to know where she is."

Babe said, "Tom, she asked me not to tell anybody. That's all she kept saying, please don't call a doctor or anybody. And I promised I wouldn't."

"Of course you did." He sighed. "Now promise *me* something. That she'll be out of here and on her way before we have a baby or an irate husband on our hands. Or both."

Babe put her fingers to her mouth, but more news slid out from under them. "I looked in her purse. It's empty, all right. Three pennies. And her name's Miller. Mrs. Kell Miller, from Kansas City."

"Babe, you're not supposed to look in people's purses."

"Well, I'm not giving a room to some kind of con girl."

Tom said, "Sweetheart, you read too many magazines. Her husband's probably looking all over town right now, trying to find her. She could be —" He started to twirl his finger at the side of his head, but his eyes met Salty's and he dropped his hand.

"She's not crazy," Salty said evenly. She had sat on broken glass, but that was her business. "She was just hungry and worried about something."

Hardy said, "How about if I nose around the sheriff's office and see if anybody's looking for lost ladies?" Tom shrugged and gave up. "Want to come with me, Rosie?" Hardy turned to Rose Ann, but she was gone.

"Can I come?" Salty asked.

"No," Tom said. "Another trip like that and you'd bring home a sick cat and two escaped convicts for us to take care of. Go give that damn gander some weeds."

As Salty clumped past Babe, she stuck out the tray to stop him, and slid her hand into his overall pocket. For a horrible moment he thought she was checking for underwear, but she drew out the coins she had given him and said, "Hardy, while you're down there, get the wax." She looked up the stairs. "Somebody might ought to sit with her awhile. In case. Rose Ann, honey —" Like Hardy, she looked around.

"She's out on the porch where it's cooler," Hardy said.

"I'll sit with her," Salty offered. Nobody heard.

Babe asked, "Is something bothering Rose Ann?"

Hardy made a wry face. "A little shaken up, maybe. Seeing what she's going to be like in about six months."

Babe's face swelled like a harvest moon. "I just knew it. I told Tom." She grabbed Hardy in her arms. "Oh, it's just wonderful. I can't get over it. A baby."

Tom disconnected Babe so that Hardy could breathe. "Don't let him fool you again, Babe. He may have ordered it out of that joke and trick catalogue."

Salty's imagination seized the idea. An exploding baby. Or, no, one that melted when you washed it. Or was really a balloon you could let the air out of and put in a drawer when it cried.

"Can I go tell Rose Ann we know?" Babe asked.

Hardy flushed. "Maybe later. We had kind of a hard night. After she told me. Talking."

"Mixed feelings?" Tom said in a careful voice.

"Ranging from gloom to doom. How it happened when we were being so damn careful is beyond me. But it did."

"Oh, Hardy," Babe said. "Don't be angry about it. It's the very best thing that could happen."

"Oh, sure. If your marriage is in trouble, complicate it some more and it'll work out just great. Good logic, Babe. But I notice you two never complicated *your* lives by —" He skidded to a stop, seeing that he had headed the wrong way.

"By having children?" Babe finished. The moon of her face slid behind a cloud.

"I used to tell her, one baby is all I need," Tom said, looking away. "One Babe."

"Not that we didn't try." Babe quirked her soft mouth into a smile. "Maybe we weren't meant." She saw Salty and scooped him out with the tray. "Go weed your duck, for goodness sake, like Tom said."

CHAPTER SEVEN

Doing the dishes had done Mam a world of good. While Salty told her about bringing home the mysterious guest, she kept nodding and smiling, even at the wrong places. Then she began to fumble in her pocket and stump around the room with her cane, mumbling, "No suitcase or nothing? What can I give her?" She opened an empty drawer. "It makes me so mad. Nothing's left. I've give myself away."

"Say her some prayers," he suggested.

"That bad, is it?"

"Can't hurt."

"You're a little heathen," Mam said, thumping his ear. "But you know a good gift for somebody, just the same. And the good Lord knew what He was doing when He sent you down that street where she was."

Tom started to pass Salty in the hall, but stopped and asked if he had ever used a lawn mower. He hadn't, but it sounded like a better job than peeling potatoes, so he said, "I think so."

"Try the front yard, then," Tom said, and hurried on.

Salty went out the front door, checking to see if he had chipped the chalk doorstop the night before, but so many bumbling feet had hit it that he couldn't tell. Out on the porch, Hardy was leaning over Rose Ann in the swing, saying, "What do you mean? I never said I'm angry. If I am it's at fate, not you. We tried our best. Didn't we?"

"I know," she said. "I know, but still —" She clamped her arms around his neck like someone being rescued. "You were so happy the way we were. That's all I meant."

The lawn mower stood in the middle of the yard where Tom had left it when all the excitement started. The catcher was full, so Salty emptied it in Tolly's pen. While he mowed, the kids from across the street chased each other with a garden hose. They looked so cool with their hair plastered and their skin shining wet that his tongue curled up like fried bacon. They skittered closer, showing off, pretending not to notice him. He hoped the ginger-haired girl had a memory as short as she was.

Tom passed again, still so busy he didn't have time to meet Salty's eyes, and said curtly, "If it'll make it any easier for you, you don't have to grind up every stick and stone and wet Eversole you come to."

Salty pulled out the tree twigs that were jamming the reel, and clattered on. A moment later a scrap of binder twine wrapped itself around the axle.

Tom gestured him back irritably and cut the twine away with a worn-slick Barlow knife. His hands with their big, warped knuckles shook. "What else do you think you know how to do? Can you wash down the porch and sidewalk without drowning half a dozen boarders?"

"Which half a dozen boarders?" Salty asked, getting the hang of Tom's sarcasm. Maybe he came from the river and had never used mowers or hoses, but he didn't have to take getting razzed. Before he could help himself, he said, "I'm trying to do things right. And go by your rules. Can't you like me?"

Tom set his mouth and began to mow.

When Salty brought the hose around to the porch, Hardy and Rose Ann were still whispering in the swing. They lifted their feet as he swished the floor with a stream of water. When he yanked the hose to reach the last corner, it hung on the porch step, and a zigzagging jet caught Hardy between the shoulder blades.

"Gaaa!" he yelled. Rose Ann leaped up. To miss soaking her, Salty swung the hose around and watered the parlor rug through an open window. Hardy doubled up in silent laughter. Then he pretended to open an umbrella and guided Rose Ann into the house under its invisible shelter.

Salty gave the rest of the floor a lick and a promise and hosed the grass clippings down the sidewalk to the gutter. When he looked up, the wet kids were watching. The one called Idalee marched up to him, dribbling a trail of drops from the seat of her bathing suit.

"Don't you squirt me," she cautioned. Salty urged the water off into the gutter, carefully coming close to her goose-bumpy legs. Brightly she asked, "Are you a bastid?"

He took his thumb off the hose to hear better. "What?"

"My mother says you're that hired girl's bastid and for me not to play with you." She had raised her voice to oblige him, and it bumbled inside his head like a rock in a kettle. He felt water filling his shoe, but he couldn't move. He knew what she was trying to say. At school a boy had called him that word and got his teeth knocked loose. He wasn't sure what to do when it was a girl, but he was about to do it.

Just as he dropped the hose and jammed his fingers into fists, Tom said from the side yard, "Idalee, leave him alone. He's busy."

They both jerked around, startled at being observed. Nothing in Tom's face showed whether he had been listening as carefully as he had been watching.

"What's a bastid?" she countered.

"No such word," Tom said. "Scat."

She flounced around as smartly as she could in her rump-sprung bathing suit and crossed the street to the others. Tom turned off Salty's hose.

"There is such a word," Salty said, holding his arm over the cramp it made in him.

For the first time, their eyes actually met and held, as intently as Indian wrestlers, while he waited for Tom to grin and make it all a joke. But Tom's eyes, deep in their sockets like well-water reflecting the sky, held him in a careful, angry gaze until he looked away. "There isn't such a word," Tom said. "But she was close." He pushed the mower off on another swath.

"I'm going to have the name I'm due," Salty said.

Tom stopped. Without turning he said, "You have a good name. Your mother gave you a name you can be proud of."

"I want his," Salty said. "Even if he didn't think I was much. They have to put it down in the courthouse or some-place. When somebody's born."

"No, they don't," Tom said to the grass. "Don't push it, Salty. Records are dead — they can't ever tell it all." He bent over the mower again.

Babe came to the front door and beckoned Salty in to help with dinner. He tried to guess if she had heard them, but she only motioned him back to the kitchen, holding her greasy fingers daintily apart.

While he was cleaning up afterward, he saw Hardy come back from town. He wanted to ask what he had found out, but by the time he finished, Hardy had disappeared. When he checked on Mam she was sleeping in her chair, still guiding it through her dreams with a hand on each armrest. The lawn mower's steady insect click came through the shades, and with it, like a cricket, Tom coughed.

It seemed like a good time to see if the strange lady was all right, but when he tiptoed up the stairs he found Babe at the top, waxing the hall floor. She shushed him with her finger and shook her head. Behind the closed door of their room, Hardy's voice asked loudly, "Why not?" and Rose Ann's answered in exasperation, "Because!" She made it sound like the final answer to every question that was ever asked.

Babe set him to scrubbing the worn battleship-gray linoleum in the bathroom. Across the street, the Eversole kids were hunting something. "Am I getting warmer?" "Stupid, you're going to burn your hand right off." That Idalee — he should have washed her right into the gutter. Right down the street into the sewer. "Now you're getting cold. Icy." He scrubbed faster, banging his head on the basin pipes. Down in the street a small voice cried, "I don't want to play this game!"

That night, Babe came downstairs with a tray of untouched supper, saying, "She's still asleep. I turned on the little lamp so she won't be scared if she wakes up."

"How do you know she's not conning you?" Tom asked.

"You read too many newspapers," Babe said. "All those love nests and sugar daddies and gin-mill murders. She's just plain tired."

Tom went off to bed, but Salty couldn't get settled for the night. Could she be tricking them when she seemed so sincere? He slipped upstairs and tried the door leading out onto the upper porch where he had first seen Hardy. Someone had locked it, probably to keep the mattress where it belonged. Salty sighed and climbed up the trumpet vine's lattice as he had before. She was still asleep in the glow of the lamp, like a haystack in a field of snow.

As he crouched at her window, his nose griddled by the screen wire, she turned over, and her eyes opened wide. Her mouth parted next, screaming without a sound. Salty threw his hands up as if that would help her know who he was, but she scrambled off the bed so wildly that she toppled the little table, lamp and all. The room went black as the bulb cracked.

He heard her gasps of breath, then a knock, and Hardy's voice saying, "Are you all right in there?"

Her door opened. Something flew through the air toward it. The overhead light flooded on. Hardy, with soap and towel in the crook of his arm, stood poised to duck, trying at the same time to look resolute in nothing but his underwear and sling. A pillow lay at his feet, and she was set to throw another one.

"Excuse me. I was just scared you'd fallen —" He followed her sharp glance to the window. "That has got to be Salty." He eased across the room sideways, trying to drape his towel, and unlatched the screen.

Meekly, Salty swung it out on its hinges and crawled through the window. He gathered up the lamp and table. "I was just trying to see if you was all right,' he mumbled, picking up pieces of bulb.

She made that rush of sound like a laugh and slowly put the other pillow down. "It's you. I see now. I didn't know I was surrounded by well-wishers." She turned to Hardy. "I'm sorry I hit you. It was all so sudden, seeing a face —" Unexpectedly she touched Salty's cheek.

"Pretty horrifying, even in the dark," Hardy agreed, grinning as Salty jerked away in embarrassment. "You okay?"

"Yes." She smoothed her dress uncertainly. "Just weak as a dishrag, is all."

"You need to eat again," Salty said, warming to her for not being angry. "I'll bring you some supper."

"No, really," she said. "I'm not an invalid, you know — just a freeloader. Can't I tippy-toe down to the kitchen and find some corn flakes or something?"

"That's no way to grow a baby," Hardy said. "We'll warm you up a real meal without waking anybody." He tried one-handed to wind the spread from her bed around his shoulders, Indian-blanket style, but couldn't. After a moment, almost in relief, she smiled and helped him drape it. They followed him down the stairs without a sound. Salty was afraid she would ask Hardy if he were the prospective father Salty had blabbed about, but behind Hardy's back she patted her stomach and then pointed to him, questioning. Salty nodded, relieved.

In the kitchen Hardy silently drew the shades, and heated soup. They fed her leftover chicken and tapioca and prunes and cornbread. Then they all had applesauce cake and milk. As if they had finished some ritual that had bonded them in friendship, she said in a low voice, "I'm Jo. Jo Miller."

"No relation to the Joe Miller joke book, I suppose," Hardy said, softly too. "I'm Big Chief Hardy McCaslin, and your benefactor here is Salty Yeager. Welcome to the Buckley Arms."

She looked around. Rested and fed, she looked even younger than she had before. The anxiety had gone out of her eyes. "Salty," she repeated. She laid her hand hesitantly over his. To his surprise he let his lie under it, thinking how different it was from the grappling hook that had held him that morning. "Thank you for helping me."

"You had us all going there for a while. We thought you were about to miscarry," Hardy said. "Incidentally, there's nobody looking for you, around town. I checked."

Her fingers moved away slowly, dabbing the crumbs. "I appreciate what everyone's done. I hope they understand that I'll pay them." She drew a long breath. "When I can."

"They're not worried about it, Mrs. Miller. Salty says you're from Kansas City." He waited, not pushing her to explain until she was ready.

She gave Salty a faint smile that seemed to apologize for grown-up things. "I must have sounded like something from the funny farm this morning. I was about at my limit. If you hadn't come along . . ." Then she was silent a long time, trying to decide if she wanted to bear her secret alone.

"I've been hungry," Salty said softly, to help her.

She studied him. Her face went gentle. But still she hesitated.

Hardy asked, "Is there anyone you'd like us to get in touch with? Would you like to use the telephone?"

"No," she said. "Thank you. No."

"Maybe your parents?"

"Not anyone, no," she said painfully, with her little fake laugh. "My parents washed their hands of me when I married an alky cutter."

"What's that?" Salty asked.

Hardy said, "He runs a cutting plant, right? You mix water and sugar and grain alcohol with real liquor and presto — three gallons out of one."

She nodded, searching their eyes. Then she went on hesitantly, "When I first knew him, when he was bringing in Mexican hooch or stealing alcohol from government warehouses, I thought it was all very daring and romantic. But it's not. It's a very cynical, ugly way to make a living."

"Speakeasy owners buy his booze," Hardy explained.

"His, or else," she said. She got up and put leftovers silently into the icebox. For a long time she looked inside,

62

hunting something that wasn't food. "That's what this trip to Dallas was for. He had to testify at a trial. He brought me along. I was afraid to travel by car like that, but I guess he thought having me along might gain him some sympathy or something. Now I would give anything if I hadn't come."

They waited. She seemed to draw herself tight, to make herself ready to leap, trusting them to catch her. "Is your husband in trouble?" Hardy asked.

"No. That's just it. He was a witness. Against another man. Someone accused of selling a bad batch. Made with wood alcohol. The man's going to go to prison for it."

They looked at each other, puzzled. Hardy said, "Sounds fair enough."

"But I know who really made and sold that batch," she said. She had grown pale. The dark circles made a little coon mask around her eyes. "My husband did. But another man is going to serve time for it. And seven people, probably many more, who drank that stuff are going to be blind the rest of their lives."

"God," Hardy said.

She closed the icebox, shivering. "When I saw him sitting up there in that witness stand, perjuring himself —" She smoothed her belly as if the baby had cried out. "Lying to God and all those people. I couldn't watch. I ran out. I thought I'd wait in the car. He had bought a little Packard runabout and we had driven down in it. I started to open the door, and all at once, knowing that car had been bought with seven pairs of eyes . . ."

Hardy took her arm and helped her sit. They all looked at their hands laid on the table like gamblers' hands holding invisible cards.

"I just began to walk. I walked. Finally I was in front of the train station, and I went in and dumped my purse on the counter and said, 'How far will this take me?' And this is the town where I got off."

"That was last night?" Hardy said. "You just wandered around Wickwire all night?"

"I sat on a box. Behind the depot. In the dark, so I could cry. I felt such a horror. I wanted him to find out where I had gone, and come and get me. And I knew if he came, I'd scream and run. Before he touched me. I don't want him ever to touch me."

Hardy said, "Hey, you can't blame yourself for what happened."

"But I do. I was there, I was part of him. I kept thinking, How could he do that, when I loved him?"

Salty propped his eyes open. He wasn't sleepy, just tired, but he had to strain not to miss anything. They spoke with the soft evenness adults used when they switched to the special language they had learned in a country he hadn't been to yet.

"What are you going to do?" Hardy asked.

"I don't know. Maybe I've left him." She made that laugh and scrubbed her eyes that had brimmed with tears. Her chin came up. "I hope I've left him. I don't want to see him. Oh, Lord. What do I do now?"

"Stay here," Salty said.

"I don't have any money. Nothing."

"There's lots of room. And you don't eat much." She needed a place the way he did. Maybe he could work a little harder and earn her keep too. He had found her, and that made him responsible, someway.

She began to rinse their dishes, looking dazed. Salty dried. Her face reminded him of the time he had decided to learn to swim and had grabbed his nose and jumped off the trestle into water over his head.

"Stay," he said.

"Why not?" Hardy smiled. "Give yourself some time. Rest. See if you still feel the same way."

"They'll let you stay here," Salty said eagerly. "And when your baby comes, me and Mam can look after it so you can get a job and have your own money —" He sank back, remembering that the Buckley Arms could sell, and scatter them all.

"I feel like a fool," she said. "Pouring all this out. It's not your worry." She made her mouth quirk up into the mock smile she belittled herself with. "I wish I was very old and wise right now. Or very young again." She dropped her hand on Salty's shoulder. "Don't ever grow up," she advised.

Her touch, asking nothing back, was like his momma's. He stood as still as when a butterfly chose him to rest upon.

"I'm afraid he's had to, already," Hardy said.

She looked sad, then smiled at Hardy in his bedspread. "But not you."

"I'm working on it. You'll have to meet my wife in the morning — she's sleeping now."

"No children?" She gave Salty a glance.

Hardy sighed. "We're working on that, too. December, sometime." He stood up, clutching his bedspread and towel. His soap fell out on the table. Salty goggled at it. It was shaped like a very pink, round naked lady.

"He's an awful joker," he said quickly, so she would understand.

"Or an awful joke," Hardy said.

"I like awful jokes," Jo Miller said. She wrapped the pink lady in the towel, the way Hardy was wrapped. She lifted her head toward the dark outside, beyond her problems. "I hear a gander."

"That's Tollybosky," Salty said, pleased that she knew the sound.

"What lovely lungs. Do the Buckleys keep geese?"

"No, he's mine. I brought him yesterday. He feels sort of new."

She turned her tired face to him, giving him her full attention. In her stocking feet she was exactly his height. "You came just yesterday? To live here?"

He went hot under her gaze. "Well, just for temporary. They're letting me because my momma worked here for so long."

"And now you're going to be her assistant?"

He could tell she was straining to be kind and interested, but he didn't know how to answer. "I can't be. She died."

"Oh, Lord," she said. "That was stupid of me. I should have realized it was something like that."

He tried to make his face flat so her gaze would slide off. "You couldn't tell. You didn't know about it."

"I know. But I should have thought. I'm so wrapped up in myself I forget how to feel out toward anybody else."

"You would have liked his mother," Hardy said. "Even when I was younger, coming to visit here — Babe's my aunt — I would sit and watch Salty's mother. Because —" He tried to think how to put it. "I think she literally saw the good, or the love, or whatever it is, in everybody. The way gypsies are supposed to see auras around people. It was like what she was seeing was the real person, and what the rest of us were seeing . . ." He shrugged, unable to explain.

Jo turned and studied Salty, her eyes alive in the stillness of her face. "You must be a lot like her, Salty. She must have passed her magic on to you."

He ducked into his shoulders, struck silent by his own sudden memory, so different from Hardy's. The brown plait of his momma's hair, wagging, puppy-dog happy. Over her shoulder, held warm in his hand as he fell asleep. But it passed, and he said, "No. I just see plain people."

She went on smiling steadily. "No, you see with love, too." He dipped deeper into his shoulders to twitch away her words and the words of his momma crushed to a marble beside the road. She said, "You had to, this morning. When you rescued me. I could feel it when I went to sleep up there, safe in the Buckley Arms."

In spite of himself, he felt a leap of gladness. "Does that mean you're going to stay?"

"You don't give up, do you?" She made that little nervous rush of air. "Yes. I'll stay if they'll let me. Until — " She practiced one of her new bright smiles. "I've got to take a gander at that gander of yours." She handed Hardy his towel, bundled around the pink lady. "And meet your wife, and . . ." Her smile began to waver.

Salty tried to make his mouth open in a laugh, to help her. Before he could, Hardy said, "Righto. And I've got to get back to Rose Ann before she thinks I eloped with the soap."

CHAPTER EIGHT

THEY had corned beef and cabbage and beans and potatoes and cornbread and buttermilk and lemon pie for Wednesday dinner because, Babe told Salty, that was what she had cooked for Wednesday dinner since the beginning of time.

The only change was that Jo Miller came bumping slowly downstairs like a lost balloon and met Mam snailing toward the kitchen. Jo Miller took Mam's hand politely and set her down at the dining table beside the McCaslins.

Babe almost heaved a platter when she came in and saw it, but Salty had already whipped out the extra plates and chairs, so all she could do was say, "Well, now, aren't you feeling *better*."

Jo smiled, looking different from last night, like a wilted plant that had got a good soaking. She had slept through breakfast, and while everyone but Hardy craned to get their first good look at her, she craned hungrily to see which dish she should attack first.

Tom came in from the mailbox with a handful of bills and a little package. He stared at Mam unfurling her napkin like the star boarder and laid the package at Hardy's plate. From his place at the head of the table he said glumly, "News flash. Ford's upped daily wages from six to seven dollars.

War's been officially abolished forever. We've had a whole decade of prosperity. And I missed it."

Hardy said, "Government just wiped you out again, Tom?"

"He's been listening to that radio," Babe said.

Tom said, "Now some crazy gink in Washington wants to raise postage to three cents."

Jo Miller looked around in the silence. Salty could feel her strain like Mam to think how to earn her keep. "Remember that old joke?" she asked. "Moronica is so dumb, she thinks the postage stamp is a new dance."

Hardy groaned. "Well, letter." He started to take beans, but noticed Mam's hands folded for grace, and stopped in mid-scoop.

Tom sighed and said as fast as he could, "Good Lord, pardon and forgive our manysins and makeus truly thankful for these-and-all our blessings."

"Amen," Mam said.

"And deliver us from any more prosperity," Tom added, passing the corned beef.

Jo took a chunk. "And our thanks to this poor creature who gave his all, that we may have life and lunch."

Every fork stopped. Then Hardy lifted his in salute. "To the cow," he agreed. "Corned in his glory. And to all the beanlets, snatched in the bloom and innocence of their youth."

Babe said, "My stars, you two," and looked at the bowlful of dimpled little potato faces gazing up at her.

"There's a theory," Jo said shyly, "that food doesn't give us life. We give food life, by using it — turning it into us. That makes sense. I think."

Tom said, "Babe's got an even simpler theory about food That's how she loves people. She feeds them."

Salty leaned against the wall and watched, basking in noonday peace. He had already snatched hot cornbread and butter in the kitchen. His stomach purred. Their voices moved him like a leaf on the river, dip, curl, tarry. He had never heard small talk before. People acting out a play called dinner.

"Everything lives off something else," Tom said. "The government off me — taxing us out of house and home. I've got to sell this place. Or just burn it down and walk away."

"Tom!" Babe said.

Hardy said, "Come on, Tom, you were born in this house, weren't you? You can't sell."

"Watch me," Tom said. "When that paint's slapped on and that roof's fixed, it's going on the market."

"You decided?" Babe said pensively.

Tom laid down his fork and put his hand over hers. She turned her hand palm-up and held to his fingers until the anger sank out of his face. "Yes," he said.

In a small voice Rose Ann asked, "When is your baby due, Mrs. Miller?"

"It's due in a couple of weeks, unless I decide to wait till Labor Day."

"Him," Mam said. "You're carrying a boy."

"I am?" Jo asked, amazed. "How can you tell?"

"High like that, a boy," Mam said. She looked around and melted into a thaw of words under their attention. "Me and Alford, we had eight children, but just three to live. And then they was taken by mishaps and sickness all but Dovie's family, that was my oldest son. And then the flu taken them in nineteen seventeen, all but her. She had it, but she wasn't about to die with Salty on the way."

Everyone looked at him. He tried to dwindle into the wall-paper. Babe said brightly, "Well, I should say not."

"All borned in Texas," Mam said, shaking salt into her hand to gauge how much she was getting. "We come right after the Civil War, the summer we got married, for Alford to work on the railroad."

Tom said, "Who would like another slice of murdered cow?"

She didn't hear him. "But we hadn't no more than got here till some shyster, just on hearsay, shanghaied Alford to county jail. Six months. We didn't even have us a house yet. You're not supposed to go by hearsay, why, my Lord."

Tom put the corned-beef platter down and resigned himself. Salty worked his way into a corner. He had heard the story a hundred times — she couldn't be stopped. Certain worn-out puzzle pieces of her life had never been laid to rest in the right place. It seemed strange to him that those bitter moments had stayed sharp and living when the hours and years surrounding them had vanished away. But maybe hate helped keep things alive. Her alive.

"They was on the railroad crew," Mam said in her slow, savoring voice. "And the overseer, he stayed up on the hill so he could watch, and he let them go down on the Trinity River and scrabble for pecans. They divided up the sack every night and had pecans. So you can see he was a good man, even being the overseer."

"Mam," Salty begged, watching their faces setting up like custard as she made up for those solitary meals in the kitchen.

Jo asked, "How long were you and Alford married?"

"Forty-two years. Forty-two. And Salty's all that's left that I know of. The end of the line." All their eyes cut to him again. "Alford used to tell folks, either you trusted to life or you died out." All at once she held out her hand to Salty. He unglued himself from the wallpaper and came close enough to be touched. "We're not died out yet, are we, baby?"

He couldn't decide if he wanted to crawl under the table to escape their eyes or stand there tall and proud because he was the strange and miraculous last one.

"Long live Salty," Jo said, lifting her buttermilk.

Tom's elbow swept his bills to the floor. Salty bent to pick them up, but Tom waved him off and did it himself.

Jo looked around, drawing their eyes to her. "Thank you for taking me in. For letting me have this time to work out my problem. I've never been in this kind of situation before. It's scary, suddenly being responsible for myself, and another life too."

Tom said, "You sure picked a what-the-hell time and country for it."

She looked puzzled. "To have a baby?"

"To be responsible," Tom said.

Babe motioned for Salty to bring the pies for her to cut. The piece she left, almost a quarter of a pie, would be for him. He put it back in the kitchen.

When he returned, licking a swipe of meringue, Tom was saying, "I don't poke into people's lives. If you can pay you can stay, is how we used to run this place." He gave Hardy his wife's-relative look. "But personally I think we ought to let the sheriff know where you are, in case your husband is looking for you."

Jo put her trembly fingers to her mouth. Babe said, "Now, Tom. She's got enough worries."

"Everybody's got worries. Look at us. House suddenly full of hungry boarders and no money changing hands."

Hardy put down his fork with food still on it. "Good grump!" He laughed. "Tom, you'll get your money."

"I have a ring," Jo began slowly. "I can sell it."

"Oh, honey, don't mind him," Babe said. "He has hard days like this when the pain gets bad. And those prissy tax-office people sending second notices like they didn't expect the most respected man in this town to pay his bills."

"I've been thinking about it," Rose Ann told everyone. "I'm going to try to get a job."

"Don't be funny," Hardy said. "You're going to stay here and take baby lessons from Mrs. Miller."

"Don't be funny yourself," Rose Ann warned, flushing bright pink. "One of us has to meet our responsibilities."

Hardy looked at all of them, his shoulders raised and his eyes round to show his wonder at her behavior. "Well, it's not going to be you. You've got your work cut out."

Salty sidled close. "There's a Help Wanted sign at the ice dock. I saw it."

"Great," Hardy said. "Wanted. Half an iceman. I'll take it. I'll welcome it with open arm."

"Don't get so heated up," Tom said. "I'm not dunning you."

"The hell you're not."

"You have a right to," Rose Ann said calmly. "We've taken advantage here. But I know I could find work. Even a few months, until —"

"No!" Hardy yelled, laughing to keep it from seeming important. "I do the breadwinning."

"Then what do you want?" she exclaimed. "Go back and live with *my* folks?"

The hand sticking out of his bandage made a fist that he banged on the table. "I want to stay right here. So do you. What about your damn dream?"

"What dream? You mean — Oh, for heaven's sake, Hardy."

"What dream?" Babe asked, forgetting to chew.

"Her dream. Listen, she had this dream that's the bee's knees, right out of Cecil B. De Mille."

"Hardy, don't."

"No, listen, it's a peach. She dreamed you had a register here at the Buckley Arms where the guests wrote their names, a big flat book out there in the hall."

"We used to," Tom said. "When my mother was alive."

Rose Ann caught Hardy's hand that was scratching the grubby cotton and gauze beneath his splints. "Hardy, I don't want you to tell it. It's private."

"Well, she opened this book and the last guest had written his name in some kind of shiny golden ink — Isadore Wright." He halted. "Did you ever have a boarder named Isadore Wright?"

Tom and Babe looked at each other and shook their heads.

"Well, anyway, in the place on the register where it says Remarks, he had written this. Now listen. *The child from this house will change the world.*" He gazed around at their still faces. "How about that? *The child from this house will change the world.*"

Everyone chewed and swallowed and looked at him. Salty felt his fingers tingle as they had once when an owl sailed over his head on a stormy night.

"My goodness," Babe giggled uneasily, "it sounds like right out of the Bible. A prophecy."

"Well, is he?" Jo asked, smiling.

"Is he what?"

"Is he right?"

Hardy stared at her, baffled. Then his face lighted. "Izzy Wright. Aha! Is he right? Who knows? That's a great new twist. Anyway, Rose Ann dreamed it just after she knew for sure the baby was on the way. Not only do we get an unscheduled kid, we get a free, gold-plated annunciation!"

"Oh, Hardy, stop it!" Rose Ann sprang from her chair. Her face had crumpled, and she snapped it to one side so they couldn't see. "You make it sound — pompous. Do you have to make a joke out of every private thing we have?"

He stood up too, embarrassed himself and embarrassed for her. "Rosie, what did I say? Sit down and finish your pie."

"It was *our* dream!" she reminded him.

"But, Rosie, it's about this place too, and everybody here is interested." He drew her down again. "Listen, this could fill the old Buckley Arms to the rafters with little pregnant ladies trying to contribute *the child from this house*. Save the old homestead for Tom, all that."

"A small notice in the local paper —" Jo suggested.

Tom said, "Unless Mrs. Miller comes early and spikes the whole shebang."

"Oh. No," Jo said, startled. "Before these two weeks are up, I'll be —" The sentence hung unfinished, like her plans. She turned to Hardy. "I'm sure Izzy meant you."

Rose Ann started up again, but Hardy stopped her. He motioned Salty close and gestured that he wanted the package by his plate opened. She hesitated as Salty shucked the wrapper off a box. "Rosie, we promised to stick together on things, didn't we? Through dick and din? Honest and true, me and you."

Salty lifted out a pair of handcuffs. Hardy held out his good hand, nodding at Salty's questioning face. Salty snapped the toothed half-circles together around his wrist.

Hardy brought his cuffed arm close to Rose Ann's. "Now hers," he directed. He threw his broken arm against his chest like a ham actor. "We're going to be in this thing together!"

Salty felt Rose Ann flinch tight with anger. Before he knew what was happening, she twisted his own wrist around and closed the other handcuff over it. He and Hardy were locked together. As everyone burst into laughter, she grabbed the handcuff key from the box and threw it under the table.

"Now a baby isn't the only thing you're stuck with," she said, and whirled out of the room.

Salty was so astonished he lurched backward, carrying Hardy with him. They righted themselves and stood still. The laughter vanished as suddenly as Rose Ann. Hardy started off after her, remembered Salty, and said, "The key." They dived under the table together and patted the shadowy rug flowers around the chair legs and lifting feet. "Damn," he snapped, dragging Salty out with him through the door.

From the hall they heard the bedroom door slam and lock. Hardy hauled Salty up the stairs two at a time and rattled the knob. Salty's hand rattled beside it, chained to his. "No," she said, inside.

"Rose Ann, in one minute I'm going to add the price of a broken-down door to what we owe Tom. Let me in."

"Add," she said.

"Rose Ann." They listened and waited. The silence stretched out, filled with the hiss of their breath. Downstairs, Tom's voice said, "Here it is."

"You don't have the right to clown with my feelings." Her voice had gone small like a hurt animal curling up in pain. "I'm not one of your catalogue tricks, Hardy. You're worse than that orphan from the river — at least he *works* for his approval. You trick people with soap pickles and think if they laugh they love you. You're still five years old, reciting in front of all your relatives in your Little Lord Fauntleroy suit!"

He mouthed a sad smile at Salty, apologizing for her, and lifted their linked hands to indicate that she thought they had found the key and she was talking to him alone.

"Rosie. Hey, remember? We were laughing, talking about your dream in bed this morning. You were kidding about it yourself."

"But that was *us*. You didn't have to let *her* make a joke out of it."

"Honey, she wasn't making fun of us. It could be her kid, if she stays long enough — *the child from this house* — why would she make fun of that?"

She said, "You're going to be a father, Hardy. You might as well get used to it. It doesn't mean handing out rubber cigars. It means you're going to have to raise a child. Head a family. Get a job."

"Honey, as soon as my arm —"

"Hardy. You didn't work *before* you broke your arm. You never held any little job more than four months. We lived off my family, Hardy. One whole year. And now we're living off yours."

Salty tried to look so interested in his shoe toes that he couldn't be hearing what they were saying. But his eyes kept going back to Hardy's handcuffed hand hanging beside his, the strong pale motionless hand held prisoner by a curve of metal no bigger than a promise.

"I've got to have permanent things in my life. A house. You." Rose Ann's voice was as sad as if she were seeing his hand too. "I love you, Hardy. Are you there? I love you, but you scare me to death. What are we going to do?"

Hardy propped his head against the door. "Well," he said slowly, "here's what I think we're going to do, Rosie. I've thought hard about this. See if I'm right. I think we're going to have a holding-the-marriage-together baby, because you thought it would help." He traced the graining of the door with his finger. "You didn't take the precautions you said you were taking, Rosie. You tried for this baby. Hard. And all the blame-laying you're giving me is just fast-talk to hide the truth."

Behind the door, silence stretched like a winter night.

"How could you do a stupid thing like that!" he yelled.

Salty tried to think what she looked like, struck dumb by Hardy's accusation, her secret face only inches from his. They waited. The soft sounds of living filled the space left open for her answer.

Hardy straightened up and walked away to the top of the stairs, carrying Salty along. Abruptly Rose Ann opened the door, but he started down without looking back, and only Salty saw her face.

He tugged at Hardy's sleeve and grabbed the newel post to stop him. As Hardy turned back, Rose Ann stepped toward him and broke into tears. Salty lifted their hands, so that Hardy's arm opened out, and Rose Ann came into it, sobbing.

Hardy held her. Finally he whispered, "Don't cry. Try not to cry. Don't you think even a little old baby the size of a bean can feel you crying?"

She struggled to make the raw jerks of her breath slow down. "I'm not sorry," she said against his shirt front. "I'd do it again. Anything to hold you, Hardy. I think this baby can. It can, Hardy. You want it too. I saw your face when you told them the dream. I know you made fun of it so nobody would know how excited and scared you really are, to think it might be true. Your special child. Because you need it to be true, so badly."

She heard the handcuffs clink as Salty miscalculated in following Hardy's slow, withdrawing hands across her back. She turned and really saw him for the first time. For a moment Salty thought she was going to reach out and draw them both back to her. But the mask she had lifted when she thought she and Hardy were alone glided over her face.

Her cool protective voice said, "You'd better go down and get yourselves out of this fix. You look ridiculous."

CHAPTER NINE

Y ou have to try to understand Tom," Babe said, looking around carefully. She was helping Salty with the dinner dishes. "He's not angry, except at himself. It hurts him to see this place going down. Literally makes him sick. It was given to him, and he loves it. But it's too much for him to handle. You see?"

He didn't, but he nodded. He just wanted to hurry. "Maybe I could fix this roof," he said shyly. "I know how."

Babe tried to laugh. "He's always saying this place is like him. Falling apart." She turned to him, so serious that she forgot she was dripping dishwater. "What you just said — thank you. Even if nothing's going to save this old place, it's good to know somebody wants to try."

"He can't sell it," Salty said. "That's stupid. There's too many of us here. We can't just jump off, like it was a ship sinking."

She scrubbed the fat glass churn she still made her own butter in. "Well, we never have, and there's been hard times when I thought we were going under for sure. Even before my time, too, I guess. Tom helped his mother run it, after his father died. That mother — whew — you might gather she and I didn't get along too well. She was a very literary lady,

79

always a little above the rest of us. She named this place. She had big hopes for herself, and for Tom, too, when he was little, but she had to stoop to keeping boarders, married to a minister."

"Did you and Tom and her all live here together?"

She rolled her eyes. "The first nine years we were married. Then, well, the ship sprung a leak. Tom was — I don't know — we both had our troubles." She leaned against the cabinet, watching him mop the worn linoleum. Her little dumpy fingers adjusted her curls. "I thought I was in love with the choir director. I wasn't, but Tom and I — we decided to separate. I went back to the town I came from and he stayed here. He was very dejected, the war worried him and all. I think he volunteered because he really believed and hoped he'd get killed."

It was hard to think of them ever being that young. Angry or sad enough to die. But he didn't want his amazement to show, so he said, "How'd his mother run it by herself?"

"Well, she didn't." Babe smiled at him. "Your mother helped her. She had worked part-time for years, but when I left she sort of filled in, and when Tom went into the army she came and helped his mother full-time."

He tried to picture it, his momma young and wild from the river, standing where he was standing, doing the literary lady's bidding in that mountain of a house.

"About a year after that, I got a letter," Babe said. "The flu, you know, it was raging then. Tom's mother was sick and asked me to come back. So I did. Your mother had gone, she had to nurse her own folks. It was a terrible time. Tom's mother died that spring. So here I was, running this big old place the best I could."

"But he come back. You made up."

"Well, he didn't come right when the war ended. He was

in the hospital. Then he came. So thin. It just broke my heart. It was so awful that we had wasted those two years, out of pride. Wasn't it? We could have been with each other during all those bad, sad times."

She rinsed out the cup towels they had dried with and hung them over the line on the back porch. Salty watched, trying to imagine the prettiness and stubborn anger and pain she had hidden with fat.

She said, "One day your mother heard that Tom was back. Still so sick. She came to see how he was, and I said, 'Dovie, come and help me.' It had been day and night, nursing him. She could see how much I needed her. So she came. She stayed. Ten years." Babe opened the screen, to let him out. They were finished. "You know about that part. She stayed the rest of her life."

Salty went out and stared at the roof without seeing it. So that was the simple way his life had been decided. He had been a baby that day when Babe said "Help me." His momma had gone to them and left him for Mam to raise. Two words were all it took.

He shook himself and went to hunt a ladder. The shingles were probably rotten and the valleys clogged with leaves. Still, maybe some small repairs could keep it from leaking. Hardy had been working on a church roof when he fell — maybe he could help. There had to be a lot of things they could do to improve the place so much that Tom would change his mind about selling.

And if improvements attracted buyers, he'd have to risk it, because they'd also attract paying guests. He wasn't just thinking of himself and Mam now, but Jo and her baby too. And if Izzy Wright hadn't meant her, then there was Hardy and the bean to think about.

Babe's story had surprised him. It was like seeing only the

backs of people, and then, when they turned around, seeing that they had different faces from what he had expected. Seeing Tom from Babe's point of view took some getting used to. She didn't see the same Tom he did, who hid what he really felt behind sour comments and said no because everyone else was saying yes. He thought maybe her Tom would have been easier to like than the real one. Maybe her Tom could have liked him easier too.

Just as he spied the ladder behind the garage, Tom walked out toward the garden. He'd have to wait. As if he were doing an errand for Babe, he got a tow sack and filled it purposefully with cans from the pile in the alley. He found tin snips in the garage and went to hunt Jo.

She was on the front porch, surrounded by Eversoles. Idalee sat beside her on the swing, wearing an Indian war bonnet of ragged turkey feathers. Next to Idalee was Eversole number two, and on the rail, tucked among the trumpet-vine leaves, were three more. From each head a construction-paper feather rose like the tail of a Halloween cat.

He set down his sack, wishing they would leave so he could get on with his plans.

Idalee said, "We're going to summer Bible school to learn all about God."

"Looking like that?" he asked before he thought. He wondered how they would know when they had learned everything.

Eversole number two piped up in a wispy little voice that matched her hair, "I already know the Ten Commandments."

"Go cook a radish," Idalee said. "You don't neither."

"I do." She fanned out her skinny fingers to count off. "Be nice. Don't make anybody cry. Mind your mother. Don't laugh about God. Don't leave anybody out. Play nice."

"You said that," Idalee sniffed. "You don't know the Ten

Commandments. You didn't say about don't comment on adultery."

"I wasn't through," Second Eversole said, puckering up to argue. Salty wished he could poke his hands in his pockets and reel off the whole list, word perfect. But the only one that actually sprang to mind was *Thou shalt not kill,* and Idalee had been doing her best to make him break that one.

Suddenly Mr. Eversole's voice went off like a cannon across the street. "Get home!" All the Indians leaped. "Stay away from there!" They scrambled off the porch, forgetting the littlest papoose on the porch rail. Jo lifted him down. He flipped out of her hands like a minnow and darted after the others, leaving her holding a bent paper feather.

"At least you have a nearby tribe to play with."

"Ugh," he said, and unexpectedly laughed too. He didn't have to hesitate with her. He made his sack clank. "I'm going to fix up this place. So good, Tom won't sell it. So nice that lots of tourists and boarders will come."

As he expected, she looked around without surprise. "Patch the sidewalk, that's the first thing they see. So they won't break a leg stepping out of their cars. The roof leaks."

"Me and Hardy can fix it. You want to flatten cans? We'll stick them under where the shingles are split."

She said eagerly, "Sure. And I was noticing that hole there in the screen. I can fix that with some fine wire, like darning a sock."

"The day I come, he asked if I could paint." Salty ran his hand over the scarred, heat-cracked walls. "I can. I'll put it on. Even just across the front would help. And thin these vines some."

She said softly, "You want him to keep it, don't you, Salty? You want to live here."

"I promised my momma I'd take care of Mam, and I don't

know no other way. But he keeps talking about selling." He shrugged. "Don't you want to stay? Specially now?"

"You mean the dream?" She smiled and began to set out cans.

"That would be something, wouldn't it? To change the world." He tried to think what that meant. Really changing the face of the earth. Like a new way of farming, maybe. Or cities floating in the ocean. Or people never getting sick or old.

"Maybe the dream meant you," she said.

He felt a little flip-flop of surprise, then sadness. "I'm not no child. But yours could be the one. Don't you want to stay and give yours the chance?"

She pressed her lips together, glancing involuntarily at a passing car. "I don't know what I want. Just to stay numb, I guess."

Babe came out. "Tom and I are going to get groceries." She got into the car when Tom backed out of the garage.

Jo stood up after they were gone and braced her back with her hands. "How about washing that light globe so at night we'll look inviting for the tourists?"

He took it down and washed it. Then he reset the slab of sidewalk that tree roots had tilted. Jo finished cutting cans and began to trim away the smothering vines that darkened the front porch. The flicker of excitement inside Salty began to blaze.

Hardy came out, rumpled and wan. While he was saying, "Who are you expecting for a visit — God?" they put a rag in his hand and set him to washing windows.

Rose Ann came down in her bathrobe and looked at them from the door. "Did you forget you were going to bring up some lemonade?"

Hardy threw his rag straight up. "I was shanghaied into this work crew just like Salty's great-grandpappy." He started to dry his hands.

"Never mind. I found some in the kitchen." She went back inside. Salty could hear her, far away, playing the sweet, slow records on the Victrola that she and Hardy had danced to, before the dream.

Babe and Tom drove up. They got out and looked at the Buckley Arms.

"What did you do?" Babe asked. "Something's different."

"Nonsense." Hardy brought the fingertips of his good and bad hands together in a parson's pose. "You're just seeing it anew through the eyes of faith, Sister Buckley."

They all went in except Tom and Salty. Tom held the screen, studying Salty's scratched arms and grubby knees. "Why?" he asked.

Salty shrugged. "To help. Till you can get paint."

Tom had a sack of groceries in his arm. He held out a package of gum.

Salty said in a hopeful rush, "If we fixed it up so more people come, you'd make more money and wouldn't have to sell."

Tom slowly pushed the gum into Salty's bib pocket and went in.

Just as Salty started into the kitchen to help, Mam tottered out on her wobbling cane. Her face was set like clabber.

Babe was wiping something off the linoleum. She exclaimed, "That dear old lady can't come in here and take over my kitchen, you hear me? You've got to see to it. She's impossible. My anniversary pitcher in a million pieces, salt in the iced tea. I have a right to my own kitchen! Help me up."

He gave her a tug and picked up some broken glass she had missed.

"Talk to her, Salty. I can't have any more of this."

"Yes ma'm." He avoided her eyes, not sure which side he was on. "She don't mean to make trouble."

"It's bad enough she sits in there talking a blue streak at meals and spilling things — and those disgusting cans she spits into —" She broke off. Salty knew why. Mam kept her cans hidden and Babe had just revealed that she snooped. Her round cheeks flushed.

He went to Mam's room. She was rocking fast, and tears were working their way along her wrinkles. When she saw him she wiped them away with a wet dishrag she had in her pocket.

"Are you all right?" he asked, not sure how to start.

"No," she answered. "I'm not all right. I'm old."

Her long shadow swung like a pendulum. He thought of the little cogs of her mind moving her, one tooth at a time, through her life.

"You're not old, Mam. You get around really good."

"I don't do nothing good anymore." She scratched at a dribble of last night's supper on her front. "I do everything wrong. It makes me so mad I could walk through a brick wall. I want to keep house and be in on things. What does she think I am? Winter clothes, folded up in here? Add a few mothballs and close the door?"

"She's just used to doing everything her own way," he told her, dabbing around her buttons with the dishrag.

"So am I. I had my own kitchen when she was chewing a rattle."

He tried to coax out a smile. "I do everything wrong, too. She yells at me like that. She gets over it."

"She gets over you because she can get good fast work out of you. I don't think she's going to get over me."

They looked up and saw Jo at the door, coming to take Mam to supper.

Mam began to shake her head, but Jo said, "Now, come on, great-grammy. I heard what you said. Phooey. Do you think you have to be useful to be valuable?" She eased Mam out of her chair, tucking wisps of her hair back into her knot as she inched her toward the door. "Will you sit by me? I want to hear more about you and Alford. And the Civil War and everything."

They crept down the hall, Jo and Salty matching Mam's turtle steps. Salty didn't know how Jo could be so patient. He could hardly stop himself from pushing ahead of them and getting on with his day. He knew Jo was right. Mam couldn't help being old. But he couldn't help being young, either, or help feeling two ways about her.

He loved her. She was his roots, the gristle that tied him to those tintype faces in her keepsake box, all dim and blurry like the past. But right now, with his muscles bunched to hurry, her slowness and feebleness galled him like Hardy's handcuffs. He hated trying to understand her griefs and move at her speed and remember she was there, in the hustle of his life. But he walked behind the wagging hem of her dress, inch after inch, practicing for the unimaginable time when he would be like that.

Tom was gone when they sat down.

All through supper their eyes kept turning to his empty chair. Babe served the meatloaf and didn't offer to explain. They talked awhile about what they could work on next day without materials, but it wasn't much.

In the silence, Hardy tried to tease the small, fixed smile off Rose Ann's face. "What," he asked the others, "can you do with a woman who just sits like a photograph saying cheese?"

"Cracker," Jo said.

"Crackers?" Babe jolted out of her thoughts. "Salty, will you get —"

"Crack *her*. It's a game," Salty said, turning back to it.

Hardy said, "But what if she suddenly begins to rant in a vilely drunken manner?"

"Stopper?" Jo asked.

"Liquor!" Salty exclaimed, forgetting himself.

"Correcto!" Hardy curved his shoulders villainously. "But what if she continues spouting gutter language?"

"Sewer," Jo laughed.

Rose Ann held her little pale smile. Babe shook her head at their foolishness. Hardy leaned and put his hand on Rose Ann's bent neck. Sadly he asked, "Can't I make you laugh?"

She squeezed her eyes shut and shook her head.

"But I can make you cry."

"Izzy Wright," Jo said kindly. "Right?"

Rose Ann said, "I want this baby. I do. But I think about that dream. Yes."

"Do you have psychic dreams very often?" Jo asked.

"What's that?" Salty wanted to know, passing ice cream.

"Oh, dreaming something, and then it really happens, like being warned of a danger. Or dreaming of a place and then actually going to that place later."

"Wow," he breathed, thinking of the possibilities.

"I have one dream," Rose Ann said. "Over and over." Her eyes drifted across their faces that had laughed at dinner. "It's stupid, with everything booming and prosperous. But I dream about hard times coming. And it's scary. There's no food. Or sunlight. It's gray, cold gray, and I hear children making little thin cries. And when I wake up, it's my cries." Her anxious eyes stopped on Hardy, and Salty thought of the first time he had seen her, up on the porch, caught in the clutch of her dream. "Things aren't going to change like that, are they?"

Hardy said, "Everything changes."

"But times aren't going to be bad for my child. The good times will go on and on, won't they?"

"Rosie — come on." He rubbed her back uncertainly. "You get to have this marvelous kid changing the world. Do you want guaranteed prosperity, too?"

"But that's just it," she said. " 'Change the world' doesn't automatically mean someone good and wise doing beautiful things. 'Change the world' could mean" — she shivered — "something terrible. Someone with a sick mind, starting another war."

"My stars, sugar," Babe reminded her. "It's just a dream."

Jo said, "There's something even scarier to think about: that we all change the world, just by being in it. Change it just by mistake, or chance. Just through ignorance and indifference, without even trying."

"But I'll be his mother," Rose Ann said. "I'll be responsible for keeping him healthy and loving him and guiding him. If I fail —"

"Hey," Hardy broke in. "Remember me? I'll be slaving away at this parent business right along with you."

She gazed at him in a long, tight-stretching silence. "Yes," she said. "You will."

Tom's car passed the window. Babe signaled Salty to fill his plate.

They followed Tom's slow, heavy steps through the kitchen. He stopped at the door. Small gasps of surprise broke from all of them. He had a gallon of paint and a parcel under one arm. He dropped a great metal-banded bundle of shingles to the floor with a crack, and the smell of cedar filled the room.

Tom's tired face quirked into a smile of triumph. He looked at Salty. "Go to it," he said jubilantly and heaved the can of paint at him.

Babe screamed for what would happen if Salty missed, but Salty's hands shot out calmly and snatched the flying can down against his chest. He set it on the table. His fingers stung. Pride and elation burned his face. Tom had trusted him to catch it. Tom had known he could and had made him prove it before everybody. A laugh burst out of him.

"Credit," Tom said, "is a beautiful invention."

"He got a job this afternoon," Babe said, making an uncertain smile.

"What kind?" Jo asked.

Tom looked at Hardy. "The one you didn't want. At the ice dock."

"You?" Hardy asked. "You're going to hustle ice?" He tore open the sack Tom handed him. Inside were brushes and a paint scraper. Hardy grinned and scraped sugar off the crust of Babe's blackberry cobbler. When she squealed, he dipped a brush in the sugar bowl and painted more back on. Rose Ann stared at him, exactly as he had gazed, perplexed, at her that morning she had slept in the sunshine.

Babe hovered over Tom's chair. "Would you rather have milk than coffee? You're going to need all your strength, Tom. You don't realize how heavy those blocks —"

"I realize," he said matter-of-factly. "I'll be as sore as a boil tomorrow night. With a whole team of charley horses." He lifted his coffee cup solemnly to Salty. "But here's to the Buckley Arms."

Everyone hoisted cups and glasses. Salty grabbed the cream

pitcher and toasted too. It wasn't the thing Tom would say about a house he was going to sell.

Tom stirred his coffee with a quiet smile. He started to sip a spoonful, but the bowl of Hardy's trick spoon had melted away, and all he had was the handle.

It was still light enough to get the ladder and climb up on the roof. Salty and Hardy hunted out the broken shingles that let rain trickle under instead of running off, and tapped Jo's flattened tin under them while Tom finished his supper. Salty scrambled barefooted over the still-warm slopes and ridges, but Hardy went slower, silent and careful. Salty suddenly realized that Hardy's fall from the church had been worse than he made out, and the sheen of sweat on his face was fear.

Up there it was like flying. Salty had never been so high, except at the courthouse when he helped Mam climb the stairs to pay her poll tax. This was better, with wind and the last of the sun striking him, and his toes tingling. Roofs tilted all around him. He could look into yards and windows. From up there he could see the shapes of things. Things he could help to change. They were going to make this place proud again. Tom had bought materials with his first money. Money he could have stuffed into Salty's hand as he bundled him and Mam off on a bus for someplace else.

Tom came out and looked up at them a long time. Then he went to the garden and knelt on the long mat of his shadow to pull an armload of beets for Babe to pickle for winter. Will I be here to eat those? Salty wondered. Winter seemed as far away as the ground.

When they ran out of tin they scraped the matted pecan leaves out of the valleys. In the last light, they pruned the fingers of wisteria and silver-lace vine and Virginia creeper that were lifting the shingles along the roof edge. Tom got a rake and grimly heaped up the prunings they dropped to the ground.

"Is he mad because we're cutting this stuff?" Salty whispered.

"Could be," Hardy murmured back. "Once he got to talking about the time he was in the hospital. He said he knew he could get well if he could just come home and lie under his trees and touch his grass again. Maybe that's why he lets everything grow so big and heavy. Like Samson's hair."

"But it's too smothery thick. Like down there over the windows of their room. It cuts off all the light."

Hardy squinted out over the housetops toward the yellow twilight that hid the river. "Keep pushing him. Maybe he'll let you prune that too. Someday."

CHAPTER TEN

Even before Tom drove off to the ice dock the next morning, Salty and Hardy were on the front porch, scraping flaky walls and nailing loose boards so they could start painting. They sang. Hardy taught Salty the words to "Making Whoopee" and "When You Know You're Not Forgotten by the One You Can't Forget," humming where he couldn't remember.

Babe came out and sat in the swing. They yelled a fine version of "I'll See You in C-U-B-A," raining paint flakes down on her, but she gazed past them with a kewpie-doll smile, deep in her thoughts.

Suddenly she asked, "Salty, will you help him? Tom? He coughed all night. This job is going to make him sick."

Hardy slumped against the wall. "You want me to go?"

"Well, I think he'd notice if you went. Don't be sensitive about not taking the job yourself, sugar. He wanted it. I couldn't stop him. But I just thought Salty might pretend selling ice was too interesting to miss."

"But it's not," Salty said. In another hour they could begin to paint.

"I know, but . . ." Babe swung with little chain-squeaks, looking at her fingers. A mockingbird, to show off, stood on the highest twig of the pecan tree and recited everything it knew.

Salty sighed. "I'll go." He banged one last row of loose nails and handed the hammer regretfully to Hardy.

"Why don't we both get back to this later?" Hardy said. "I've got things to do, too."

Salty told Mam where he was going, slapped down his cowlick, and trudged off.

The ice house was new. He had watched it being built. Ice from the plant across town was trucked to it, so that people could drive up in their cars and take home ice for their ice boxes.

There were no cars when he walked up. Tom was in a cubbyhole of an office, counting change. Salty had a good idea of what Babe expected. "This looks like more fun than doing dishes," he said dutifully.

Tom swiveled around in his chair. Surprise, then something like pleasure, flashed across his face. But he said with cool carefulness, "I thought you'd be painting."

Salty gave his hand an airy flick. "Hardy had something else to do. So I have this free time." He looked around. Next to the heavy door of the storage room was a little chute with handles beside it. He knew how it worked. Pull one and a twenty-five-pound block of ice slid out. Pull another for fifty pounds. He used to know just the moment to grab a broken hunk of ice and run.

A fellow in a banged-up Ford truck turned in and wanted a hundred-pound block for his fish-bait store.

"How about two fifties?" Tom asked hopefully.

"Hunnerd lasts better," the fellow said.

Tom sighed and pulled a lever. He caught the great, crackling block with his tongs as it slithered out under the canvas flap. Before Salty could think, he grabbed a pair of tongs, too, and together they struggled until the ice rested on a blanket in the back of the truck. They packed another blanket over it. The truck rattled off.

Tom looked embarrassed. "Wouldn't have been so heavy if it wasn't so damn slick." But he hung his and Salty's tongs on the same nail.

They worked together till nearly noon. When Tom learned that Salty wasn't needed even then at the Buckley Arms, he fished in his pocket for dimes and sent him to the grocery store for cheese and crackers and grape soda pop and a can of salmon. While Salty was waiting for it to be sacked, he shyly studied the punch board on the counter. Under one of those little circles was a lucky number that could bring him a prize. He licked his lip, hungry for something more than lunch. One of the prizes was a Barlow knife. Like Tom's.

After they ate, Tom swung open the heavy door and they went in where the ice was kept. Frosted coils looped back and forth across the ceiling. Their breath clouded in the sudden cold. Tom went to a corner behind the looming blocks of ice. "How about this for dessert?" he asked, bringing out a watermelon the size of a torpedo. "Fellow brought a load from down south and left some here to cool for a picnic, but this one cracked. Do you think you and I . . ."

"Sure we can," Salty said in a frozen puff. He staggered when Tom put the striped giant into his arms. Tom scraped a tin cup along the frosty coils until it was heaped with ice crystals.

"Pour the rest of your soda pop over this."

"Is that a snow cone?" Salty marveled. "I never got to taste one before."

"No?" Tom asked. "Well. Now you get to."

They ate watermelon until their breath wheezed and their fingers stuck together with pink juice. When a load of cotton choppers came by to ice their water barrel, Tom had to prize himself up, groaning.

Mr. Eversole drove up. After Salty wrapped his fifty pounds in newspaper and tugged it onto the floor of his Model T, Tom sent the last wedge of watermelon back to the Buckley Arms with him, for Babe.

A little kid came for twelve-and-a-half pounds. He talked nonstop while Tom chipped a twenty-five-pound block in two with his pick. Tom teased right back, laughing as he tied twine around the chunk and set it in the kid's red wagon. Salty watched, longing for power like that to make Tom laugh.

He was sweeping their watermelon seeds up to take home when Tom said, "Damn. I locked the keys up in the engine room." They each yanked the door of the small room to be sure and stood thinking what to do. "I could drive back to the plant for another set, if you think you could hold down the fort."

"I maybe could squeeze through that little window and open the door from inside," Salty said. "If you'll boost me."

They went around to the side. Tom knelt on one knee and Salty stepped up on the other, stretching to wrench the narrow window open. With a shove from Tom he got his head inside, gripping the window ledge, and squeezed his shoulders through. He began to rattle with the vibrating engine just below him. The hot oiliness of the air in the tight room sucked his breath away. He caught at a throbbing pipe in the dimness so he could pull himself the rest of the way in, but it was hot. He snatched his hand back.

"Stuck?" Tom's muffled voice asked.

"No. Just — can you give my feet a shove?"

He felt Tom's hands pushing against his sneaker soles. He twisted until he was almost sitting in the thin slit of window.

96

His hands groped along the greasy wall for something to hold on to. A kind of warm, metallic box protruded. He clamped his hand over it.

Instantly his nerve ends flared like lightning. A spasm locked him in rigid, impossible pain. He blazed in silence until he felt himself jerked out into light and life again.

"Oh, my Lord." Tom was bending over him when he opened his eyes. He was on the ground, and they both shook as though the engine still thundered through them. "Are you all right?" Tom's face was as gray as ice. "You grabbed the switch, Salty. My Lord, you could have —"

Salty felt hard arms gather him up and hold him like a vise. His nose mashed into the fat, marbled fountain pen in Tom's shirt pocket.

"I'm all right," he whispered shakily. He felt like a ghost. Transparent. All his strength had sizzled away. "What was it?"

"A shock. You just took two hundred and twenty volts of electricity."

"I did?" He breathed awhile, shivering with cold sweat in the oven-hot air. He arranged Tom's words in his mind. He supposed that was a lot of volts. He guessed Tom had saved his life. He had to thank him, but all he wanted was to lie there without moving, ever, with his head against Tom's chest.

"I'm sorry," Tom mumbled, more a movement than a sound. "My Lord. Why didn't I *think* —" His rough hand scraped over Salty's hair. "Warned you about it. I wouldn't let you get hurt for the world. You know that, don't you?"

Salty opened his eyes again. A car was stopping. "I'm all right," he insisted, and noticed he had been holding Tom as tightly as Tom had been holding him.

He rested awhile, still dazed, while Tom sold ice, but was helping again by the time Hardy came walking up and asked how they were doing. Tom and Salty exchanged glances, and Salty saw that it was going to be their secret.

"You two tycoons think you're smart?" Hardy asked, tilting his hat back. "I got a job too." He enjoyed their surprise a moment. "Feeney's Bakery. Starting tonight. I'm going to knead dough in the cold, gray dawn because I need dough for the cold, gray rent. I'm even going to drive the pie truck."

"With one hand?" Tom asked.

"Feeney left an arm in France, and he drives it. He says I can."

Salty grinned at him proudly, wondering if Hardy would get to bring home leftovers the way his momma brought things from Babe's kitchen.

"So," Hardy said, with one of his actor sighs, "I invited my Rosie Annie to a matinee to celebrate and she said what's to celebrate and we got snippy and I walked out and how would you like to go swoon over Theda Bara?"

Salty asked Tom with his eyes, torn between going and staying. Tom said, "Better make that Hoot Gibson and a bunch of hoss thieves."

"Do my best." Hardy wrapped a chip of ice in his handkerchief — his real handkerchief — and wiped Salty's juicy face. "What turned you so white around the gills?"

"Too much watermelon, maybe," Salty said, watching Tom.

"Go," Tom said. The cool carefulness had come back into his voice. "Just remember, get yourself home to help fix supper." He began to cough, and turned away.

Hesitantly Salty followed Hardy down off the dock. It was over, the closeness. Maybe he had imagined it, or blown himself out the window so it could happen.

They headed for the Pictorium. Salty watched as Hardy

rolled a cigarette one-handed like a cowboy. "Why are we going to the show instead of getting back to the painting?"

"The sooner we paint, the sooner Tom sells and out we all go." Hardy's cigarette was so crooked he threw it at a fire-plug. The tobacco spurted in all directions, the way all of them at the Buckley Arms would scatter if Tom sold it. Salty drooped. He had been sure Tom was repairing the house for staying, not selling. "No, the real reason is, I needed to get away. She bawled me out about the job: 'Hardy, it's at night!' Scream, scream. 'Hardy, we should have talked it over before you took it. Hardy, get a job — but not that one.' Whew."

Salty stopped in his tracks. Through his mind a face had flashed an instant, anxious and drawn. Tom's. No, but almost. Only, how could he know? It was years ago, and hadn't he been asleep?

"What?" Hardy asked.

"Nothing." They went on. Carefully he said, "Could we go to the courthouse instead of doing this?"

"What for?"

Instantly he was sorry he had mentioned it. It was some-thing he had to do by himself. For himself. "I was just kid-ding. Are you really going to make bread?"

"What else is left? Flagpole-sitting? Winning a yo-yo mara-thon? Roller-skating to California and being a movie star?"

Salty cackled. He knew Hardy was joking. There was Rose Ann to take care of. And the bean.

They stopped before the posters outside the Pictorium. A spit-curled vamp was getting her neck kissed by a man with patent-leather hair. "You go for this sheik and sheba stuff?" Hardy asked.

Salty shrugged, wishing it could have been Buck Jones

and Silver. "Sure, I guess." The warm smell of popcorn drew them in.

The theater had been wired for sound, but Salty heard only the organ down front, so it wasn't a talkie. They bounded up to the balcony. It was empty except for an old oiled guy nipping forty-rod from his hollow cane. On the screen a busty lady was talking on the phone in a boudoir. A French maid overheard something awful and made a horrified mouth. She rushed out, jouncing the bow of her baby apron.

It wasn't Salty's kind of movie. He felt strange, taking Rose Ann's place. She would have liked it. He whispered, "Maybe you should've asked her again, nicer."

Hardy sighed. He opened a roll of Wint-o-green and flicked a tinfoil bullet over the balcony rail.

It wasn't his business, Salty knew. He couldn't come right out and say that he had been very close to someone that day, and wished the same miracle for everybody. "Maybe you should've talked over taking a night job so it wouldn't have been such a surprise to her."

"What about the little surprise she gave me?" Hardy asked softly. "We sure as hell didn't talk that over. If she can take it on herself to have a baby, I can take it on myself to get a job to pay for it."

"Don't you want a baby?" Salty whispered. "When you and Rose Ann was arguing, she said you really did. Because of the dream."

He felt the jerk of Hardy's grunt. "The bean that changed the world? Sure, maybe I would have, if it had just happened. But I resent being tricked, damn it. I don't like strings on me. I want to stay married because I want to, not because I've got a kid to raise."

He wished Hardy wouldn't say that about the bean, when

being wanted was so lovely, but he watched the flickering screen and was silent.

"It's not the kid's fault." Hardy made a wintergreen sigh and passed the roll to Salty. "I wanted kids someday. Sure. Kids are *you*. They're how you go on, down through the generations. I could love a kid. Walk to me, take a step to Daddy."

He stopped, embarrassed, and they watched the movie. Right in the middle of a kiss the screen flashed and streaked and went blank. A boo rose from downstairs. Back in the booth the film flapped itself to a halt. So did the projectionist's reel of muttered curses.

Salty gathered his courage. "Your kid's going to be lucky. I mean, with a daddy that does jokes and tricks and all. And laughs and has fun."

Hardy stared at the empty screen. "That's not enough to give him. There's so much I need to give him. To make him happy and valuable. Things I missed. Things I see you missing."

They listened to the clanking in the projection booth. The old oiled guy who shared the balcony had gone to sleep over his propped cane. In the helpful dark, Salty said, "I wish you could have been my daddy."

Hardy rearranged himself uneasily. "You'll have to settle for being Uncle Salty to my kid."

"I know," Salty said. "But . . ."

"Don't be greedy," Hardy said. "You've already got a daddy."

Salty took a breath as cold as ice-house air. "What's that mean?"

"You know what that means."

"What's it mean?" he asked, unaccountably chilled to the bone.

"Oh, come on, Salty. Quit pretending. You're a big boy now. You know things."

The screen flashed into life. But it was a cartoon. Krazy Kat was shivering in his bed because a jar of cold cream sat beside it. Down on the main floor the audience hooted and whistled. The screen went dead again.

"My daddy got killed. In the war. That's why he never come back."

"Bull, Salty. The whole crazy world died in the war. Nobody came back the same, to the same things. Not even Tom."

CHAPTER ELEVEN

SALTY gulped for air. "I don't know what you mean," he whispered.

"Come on, Salty. You're too idealistic. You can't live like you did out there on the river with your momma and Mam. Face facts."

Hardy's shoulder grazed his. He flinched away to keep from being touched. "What facts? You don't have facts."

"Salty, I read Dovie's note. Remember?"

The film started. The French maid was being chased by a handsome man in a top hat. She liked it. The organ trilled as she hid behind doors. Legs in black silk stockings. "That wasn't facts," he whispered. Inside his head, his momma's wobbly-lettered words flipped like broken film. Love him. He take you in. Love him.

"Salty, it's as near as you'll get. Nobody but Tom can give you facts, now."

"How come *you* know, then?"

"Because it made sense, right from the beginning. Why Dovie sent you and you came. Why he took you in. Tom's trying to come to terms with this thing, just like you are. He wouldn't be struggling to work out his feelings if you didn't mean something to him."

Salty shook his head. The images jumped before his fixed eyes, black, white, meaningless. The door of his memory opened again. A face looked at him. He looked back through his eyelashes, pretending to sleep.

He had been five. The hand felt his fever-hot cheek. The rough hand.

"He lied to me," he whispered.

"You mean you asked him? Straight out?"

"No, but I — I talked about my daddy. I asked him if he knew who." He began to burn with grief and anger. "And he said some stranger was." The organ rumbled. He wished for that nameless, faceless father. That soldier-boy on his way to be killed and never mentioned again. Because Tom for a father, passing him on the street all his life without wanting to love or even know him, hurt too much to stand. "He lied to me. Damn him! He's the bastard."

"Take it easy." Hardy glanced around at the empty seats. The old drunk snored. "We'll get ourselves thrown out."

"Why can't he just say who I am!"

"Because of Babe, Salty. It's not something he can tell her. He's trying other ways to make it up to you. Taking you and Mam in —"

"Why can't he admit he's my daddy? Is he ashamed of me?"

Hardy laid his good hand over Salty's knees. "What difference does it make who your father was? Or his father was? You're you."

"Did he think something was wrong with me? Because my momma didn't talk? Is that why he didn't want me?"

"Salty, the only thing wrong with you is that you're Dovie's boy, and not Babe's."

Salty stood up. "Well, that's not enough reason." He blundered down the dark stairs and out into the fire of afternoon. He had never left in the middle of a picture show before.

Hardy came clumping after him. "Salty, listen. I know it's not enough. You've got a legitimate grievance."

"What's that mean?" It sounded like a sickness.

"It means you've got a right to hate him." He looked distressed. "Salty, I'm sorry. I should've left it alone."

"Why?" Salty asked, pushing past people on the sidewalk. "I already knew about it." He almost believed he had known. Had always known. "Once he come out to our house. I was sick. I opened my eyes in the night and he was sitting there. I was just too little then. To know who he was."

He stepped out in front of a car. Hardy yanked him back and held his arm a moment, without a word.

They crossed the street into the warm smell of ocean creatures and brine. Through the fish-market window, Salty stared into the dead, astonished eye of a bullhead in a tub of ice. "I used to wish he'd come again. I'd say I had a bad bellyache. But Mam give me castor oil, and he never come." A yellow cat in the window cleaned its paws and watched him. "Did he hurt her?" he said to Hardy waiting behind him. "My momma? She loved him. Her face was pretty when he drove her home on rainy nights." The cat stood up and pressed its side against the glass, asking for a touch he couldn't give. "Did he love her?"

"Salty, it was a long time ago."

"He couldn't have. If he had, he would've done right by her."

"Salty, these things aren't that simple."

"If he loved me, he'd do right by me."

"Salty, sometimes people aren't free to do what they'd like to do. Tom's not. You're going to have to accept things the way they are. He's not going to let you mess up his life."

Salty wheeled into an alley so no one could see his face. The ocean smells dried to inland dust.

"Salty, you're going to have to strike a bargain, you and Tom. You love Mam and want her to have a place to stay. You've got a promise to keep. Tom loves Babe and he's going to keep the promises he made to her."

"Why can't he love *me?*" The blind-eyed backs of buildings rose up and cut off the sun from a slit of sky laced with wires.

"Because he needs to be loved and accepted just as much as you do. By Babe."

"How could my momma say 'love him,' then, when she knew what he was like? She didn't write *him* a note, for him to love *me.*"

They came out into another street so hot it nearly took their breath. Hardy said slowly, "Your momma knew things about love that most of us don't know. What it really is, instead of what most of us do with it. I think she wanted you to struggle with that note." He stopped at an ice-cream man's little cart and counted his pennies.

"I'm never going to love him," Salty whispered in horror. "Never. I don't care no more about him than he does me."

Hardy handed him a cone filled with two tilting scoops of chocolate ice cream. Salty turned from it and walked on. The sidewalk flared and darkened, making movie images of sun and shadow that he strode across.

Hardy came up behind him, saying, "Hey, eat this thing before it melts."

His stomach lurched. He came to a stop at the foot of the courthouse steps, but his thin shadow zigzagged up them. From the door came the smell of spittoons and justice and the dust of recorded things.

*   *   *

After they had walked in silence long enough, Hardy took Salty's arm and gently eased him home.

"It's just the heat," he told Babe when she looked up from cookie-making and saw Salty's ashen face. "He just needs to cool himself a little while."

Hardy glanced up the stairs at Rose Ann standing in the door of their room. He scooped up a deep breath and went to make up their quarrel.

Salty pushed right past Babe and out the back door. He sat with Tolly. His bones ached. All the stomach-churning anger he had shoved to the back of his mind as they started into the house began to bang steadily like prisoners wanting out. It wasn't the heat. He was sick. He had legitimate grievances. A terrible disease he had never had before, called hate.

Mam rocked at the window of her room. He guessed he ought to see if she needed anything. But he didn't move. What could he say to her? Hadn't she lied to him as surely as Tom?

Maybe that wasn't fair — maybe she never knew either. Maybe when she asked, his momma had silently pushed the pencil and paper away and kept that secret locked with all the rest.

Maybe that was where it belonged, dead with his momma.

Babe came to the kitchen door and looked out at him. He smoothed Tolly's crackling silk feathers until she went back in.

He didn't know what he could ever say to Babe. He almost liked her. He had grown up on the leftovers of the food she cooked so good. She wasn't to blame for his life. She didn't even know he had a right to part of that love Tom had given her so long.

Tolly's tiny rows of teeth gently grated his fingers. He shoved everything back into his mind again and shut the door. He couldn't be soft with Babe. She was a contradictory woman. Hadn't she already turned on Mam? When she turned on him he had to be ready.

Tolly dabbed patiently beside him with one fly-swatter foot lapped over the other, fixed to fall on his bill the first step he took. Salty stroked him, moving slowly to keep from throwing up.

He could hurt people. He had never had that kind of power before. He had lives in his hand. It scared him, in a way nothing else ever had. It might have been better if he had just died that morning. Grabbed the exposed wires of that switch in the engine room and held on till his brain fried. Never opened his eyes again or felt Tom's arms around him.

Babe called him in. As he passed her in silence she laid her hand on his hot forehead. He jerked away.

"Get a cool bath," she told him. "I'll make you a lemonade."

He went to bed in the strange, still glow of sunset. He could hear the squeak of the floor as all of them drew up their chairs for supper. He didn't know how they did it, grown people, looking ordinary while they crawled with secrets, saying the opposite of what they felt. The evening throbbed with heat. He wiggled and sweated and stared at his ceiling as it dimmed, waiting for his sickness to pass.

When a hand touched him in the night he jumped like a grasshopper. Someone bending over him blotted out the gray sky of the window.

"Salty, will you do me a favor?" It was Jo in a borrowed nightgown of Babe's, bulging like a sailboat in a gale.

"Now?" he whispered, grabbing the sheet to his chin.

"Please. I'm scared."

"Is the baby coming?" He sat up, going cold.

"No. There's a car. Parked out front, under the trees. I

can't tell exactly, it's so dark, but —" She caught her breath. "I know this sounds silly, but —"

"You want me to see if it's a Packard runabout?"

"Would you? Do you feel like it? I've got to know."

"Sure," he said, suppressing a shiver. His stomach had settled. He grabbed his overalls. "Do you think he's found you? Why would he be just waiting?"

"I don't know. It can't be him. But what if it is?"

Salty tiptoed upstairs and across the kitchen, feeling for the door. A new, cool breeze struck him as he crept around the house. He eased up to the car in the dappled tree shadows. It was a Buick, with a flat. Someone had walked on home and left it to fix in the morning.

She was sitting on his bed when he got back.

"No," he whispered.

"Oh, boy," she said in her husky voice. "Oh, boy. Thank you, Salty. I'm sorry I woke you. I couldn't get to sleep, and when I walked past my window and saw that shape out there . . ." He could hear her uneven breathing. "I thought he'd come for me."

He didn't quite know what to do. He stood at the foot of the bed trying not to be sleepy. "Maybe he won't ever find you." He balanced on the outside edges of his feet.

"He will. Something will give. It can't just hang like this."

"You still like him," he said, disappointed.

"I still love him. But I hate the kind of work he does. How the money comes. Illegal like this. I hate how it's changing us from the nice, funny people we used to be. I don't know how I'm going to explain it to this child someday."

The springs creaked sharply as she bent over and clapped her hand over a long-drawn breath.

"What is it?" He almost forgot to keep his voice low.

"Just a cramp. What they call false labor pains."

"Do you need a doctor?"

"No, I had them once before, but not for so long. It's just — sort of practicing for the real thing."

"You want me to call Babe or anything?"

"Oh, boy, that's the one thing I don't want. Rousing this house. The Buckleys would have doctors and sheriffs and Kell all pouring in here."

"You want me out?" he asked.

"Hey. No. Get back to bed. I wasn't thinking. I'll just sit here at the foot. Just a few minutes. To get my courage back."

He got shyly into bed again in his overalls, trying not to poke her with his toes.

She said, "Go back to sleep. I know you're tired, after today."

You don't know anything about this day, he thought, but he batted his eyes and said, "I'm not sleepy."

"I am." They were silent again, comfortable with each other. "Maybe we'll get a rain," she murmured. The trees said something in the wind that came off a faraway storm.

When he woke in the dark she was curled up at the foot of his bed. He thought he heard a gasp, but the trees were rustling and he wasn't sure. Maybe she was crying. She had a right to cry. He made himself into a ball to give her room.

The next time, her movements snatched him awake. She was making the grunting sounds of little boys fighting, and she was holding to the iron bars of the bed so hard the bed shook.

"Are you all right?" he whispered.

"Go to sleep." This time for sure she was crying. "I was just leaving." Then she jerked like a real fighter did when a real fist smashed into him.

"How long does this false stuff last?" he asked, scared for her.

"Not this long."

He bolted up. "You mean it's not for practice?"

"If this is practice, there's not going to be enough of me left for the real show."

"You mean the baby's coming now?" He jumped out of bed to give her room. He wasn't sure for what. "Hey, you can't just — in here —" His scalp was tingling. "What if something happens!"

"Something's supposed to, goofy child. Soon, I hope."

"But they'll say why didn't I wake them up or send for a doctor or —"

"And you're going to say I wouldn't let you." She sounded ordinary again. "Hey, this has been happening for thousands and thousands of years. Stop leaping around and let me concentrate."

He sat down uncertainly at the head of his bed. He knew people and animals and insects and everybody were being born every second. It was the most natural thing in the world. Except when it was somebody he cared about, and in his bed.

"Maybe I ought to leave. You want me to go?"

"Hey, I'll go with you," she gasped. "This is no fun." She took his hand in the grappling-hook clutch she had held him with when they were trying to get to the Buckley Arms. "Don't be scared. I'm not scared. But stay a little while." She was gasping, but she noticed and began to draw long slow gulps of air. She loosened her grip. "Just a little longer. I apologize. I made a mess of your bed. Messy. I guess. Is what I am."

"Maybe I could get Mam down here. She'd know."

"Wouldn't she, though? Eight children and three to live? No, let her rest. Lord. That's brave. Eight times."

She raised herself on her elbows, caught in a spasm. "Isn't there something?" Salty asked in distress. "Won't anything help?"

When she could, she said, "Don't think about it. I don't. I'm thinking about somebody coming who's not like anybody who ever lived. So special that I'll look back. And say. All this was worth it."

They both held to the bed like Mam guiding her rocker through her dreams. The sky was still black, but it felt close to morning. The cloud was closer, flickering with electricity.

"Do you need anything? The light on?"

"No. I'd imagine faces were peeping in. Anyway, it's not as if this kid was flying around the room and I was trying to swat it."

He went to the window and looked up at the dark slit of sky. Somebody was being born on Friday, June the twenty-eighth, nineteen twenty-nine. He wondered if that would be a date in history books some day. He wondered if something wonderful or terrible or earthshaking was beginning now, and no one knew it.

"Salty," she said in a worn voice, "I'm tired. Hardest work I ever did. Don't worry if I don't talk anymore. Go up. To porch. Get laundry basket. Everything, so we can wrap him up. Can't present him to the world. Wrapped in newspaper."

She went back to work, making the same writhing sounds as the wind-strained trees.

He threw himself up the stairs, relieved to be useful at last. He felt around the back porch for the basket. Nothing came to his hand. Then he remembered. That morning, Babe had sent him to get the clothes off the line, and he had stopped halfway across the yard to go fill Tolly's water crock.

He could see the white ghosts of laundry still flapping in the wind. He found the basket blown against the fence and began to cram the washing into it as fast as he could. If Tolly woke and honked, the whole house might wake. Babe would remember the wash and come pounding out for it. Anxiously he grabbed everything, even socks, when all he needed was baby wrappings.

He made it back to the house and let out his breath. No sounds came from the other rooms. He went down under the mountain again, where Jo was busy making history.

CHAPTER TWELVE

Before he got to his door he could hear her breathing. She was trying to push a car-size boulder up a hill. Or lift a wrecked train off her legs. Or keep from drowning in a whirlpool. He slid to the cold floor, still holding the basket, and braced his back against the wall. His first thought was to rouse Mam and set her to praying like a house on fire. But on second thought he figured he could do it faster himself. At each jerk of the springs he started over, higher and louder in his mind, Please, God, help her. Please Godhelper. Oh, damn it, help her!

Then the ragged breathing stopped and only the trees surged and rustled. He scrambled up, afraid she was dead. He forced himself to take a step into the room. She was curved protectively around something that made a small angry squall. She said back to it, "Hey, hello."

He brought the basket to her side. "Is it — did it —"

She touched him with a wet and sticky hand. "We're right here," she whispered, so tired and proud that his throat closed up. "But need to rest a few minutes." She curled again. He saw her white teeth smiling at a head like a grapefruit that she was holding in her hand.

He sat down outside the door again, leaving it open in case

she spoke. He felt her relief and thankfulness echoing in himself. He wanted to giggle and sleep and yell out the news to everybody. If Izzy Wright was right, he had just lent his room to the child who would change the world.

He guessed he had arrived like that, in a burst of pain and gladness. Or maybe only pain. He hoped, for his momma's sake, he had made up for it, or still could.

He was sleeping like a stump when Babe bent over him in the stormy morning dimness, saying, "Salty, what on earth?" Before he could untangle himself, she stepped over him into his room and let out a factory-whistle shriek.

As he bolted in at the door she bolted out, blocking him like a truck.

"No! Salty, stay out of there." He got a glimpse of Jo's face, startled awake, and the bloody stains on the bed before Babe filled the doorway. "Oh, my living stars. I can't cut a cord. How? I've got to remember everything I ever heard —" She caught his shoulders. "What is she doing down here in the *basement?*" She turned him loose as if he had scorched her. "No, I wouldn't believe it. Run upstairs. Tell Tom to bring a pan of warm water. Washcloth. String. Drop the scissors in the kettle —"

"Scissors!" he exclaimed.

"Tell Tom to bring another one of my gowns. And a clean, torn sheet."

He staggered off, reeling under her instructions. Tom was at the top of the stairs. "I heard her. Sounds like she's going into the baby business." It surprised him that Tom looked the same as yesterday. But why shouldn't he? They hurriedly gathered the things Babe asked for. Tom said, "You must have had quite a night. Why didn't you tell us what was happening?"

For the answer to everything, Salty pointed out a front

window at the Buick parked in front of the house. "She was scared. She thought her husband had found her."

"What do you mean?" Tom asked sharply.

He gulped. "That's all she said. I don't know what it means."

Tom blew out his breath. "I see."

They went down to Salty's room. Babe opened the door wide enough to take what Tom handed her and slammed it. "Stay out. Everything's fine. I'm just neatening up a little."

They stood outside the door. Tom said, "Babe would neaten the city dump." The pink lightning of an arriving storm lit them. After a thunderclap he asked, "Boy or girl?"

Salty shrugged. He hadn't thought to ask. All he wanted was for Tom to leave and let him wait alone until Jo needed him.

The baby began to squall in loud gusts of anger. Babe stuck her head out. "Tom. She needs to be back in her own room. Do you think the two of you —"

"I can carry her by myself," Tom said.

"Oh, Tom, I'd rather you didn't, the way you've been coughing."

"She can't be much heavier than a hundred pounds of ice." He went in. Salty followed. The baby was in the basket, wrapped in one of Babe's soft petticoats from the clothesline. All they could see were pink gums making a yell below squinched-up eyes. Babe picked the basket up.

"Salty can carry him," Jo said in a soft voice.

"Him?" he asked.

"Him. Just like Mam said."

Babe grudgingly let go the basket. The baby hushed. Tom lifted Jo in her clean nightgown and they started the careful climb to her room. Suddenly, with a sound like the cracking of bones, the storm hit. They climbed up through it as thunder barreled down the stairs, drowning a flurry of rain at the windows.

In his pride Salty almost forgot to breathe. He wished he could stop and show Mam, but her door was closed. He followed Tom's back, while Babe behind him reeled off endless instructions.

Tom tucked Jo into her own bed and sat down to get his breath. Jo held out her hands. Salty laid the baby, like a ticking bomb, into her arms.

Tom said, "Mrs. Miller, you took a risk. If something had happened, we could be in a mess of trouble."

Jo closed her eyes. "I'm sorry for all this. It wasn't supposed to happen so soon."

"Oh, Tom," Babe cut in, "she's young and healthy. Your mother didn't have a doctor or even a midwife. She told me a dozen times about the blizzard and you arriving a full day before the doctor got here."

"I don't mean that," Tom said. "I mean we can't be responsible for you, Mrs. Miller. Either you'll have to get in touch with your husband, or I'll have to ask the sheriff to locate him."

Jo pressed her shaking fingers to her mouth. "Please don't," she whispered. "Not yet."

Babe glared at Tom. "He won't, honey. Now don't worry. Rest."

They all looked around. Rose Ann stood in the doorway, clutching her bathrobe. For a second Salty looked for Hardy, before he remembered he was at the bakery.

Tom said, "Come over. Look what the stork brought us."

She cringed at the thunder. A gust of wind rattled the house and plastered leaves against the window. "I thought we were having a tornado, when I heard everyone moving around."

She stayed just inside the door, her eyes fixed on Jo. "We're not, are we?"

"Come and see my boy," Jo murmured.

Rose Ann drew her bathrobe closer. "I hate storms." She flinched at another lightning flash. "Aren't you scared? All alone? A baby with no father, no family, no home? Dear God, I don't want to have my baby in a rented room." The thunder clapped and she was gone.

Babe said sadly, "What possessed Hardy to take a night job, just when she needs him the most?"

They all looked in different directions, uncomfortable. In a silence they could hear a drip from the ceiling. Tom sighed. "Still some work to do up there." He brought a scrub-bucket to put under it. They listened to the plop of drops. Salty knew what had possessed Hardy. This crazy old ark of a house, and the gathered-up family that it held.

Babe arranged the basket on two chairs beside the bed and went out. When she came puffing back she opened a cardboard box on the foot of the bed and shyly held up bits of white cloth.

Jo said, "Oh, Mrs. Buckley, I couldn't."

"Oh, foot, you want him to grow up in a rayon petticoat?" She smoothed the little pieces. "They're old, but they're clean."

"What's in that box?" Tom asked.

Babe's smile shifted to carefulness. "They'll be some use to somebody, finally. I want her to use them."

Tom pulled them out of her hands. A little knitted shoe the size of his thumb fell to the floor. "You saved this junk? All these years?"

Jo said gently, "You miscarried?"

Tom crammed the things back into the box and smashed

the flaps down. The smell of dust gusted from it. "Over and over and over," he said, and went out.

Babe gazed after him. The rain-distorted light from the window trembled across her face. Then she shook herself. "Salty. Start breakfast, or he'll go to that stupid job without any. I'll be down as soon as I get this precious all snuggy in a little gown and blanket." She tried folding a diaper every which way until Jo giggled. "Do you feel up to a nice cup of tea?" she asked. "Maybe a slice of toast?"

"I'd rather have ham and eggs and a gallon of milk," Jo said. "I'm starved."

Salty went down to fix it, but he saw Tom in the kitchen, pouring coffee, and veered off to Mam's room.

"Jo has a baby. Last night we got a new baby," he told her in a proud rush. "You're right, it was a boy all along."

"Already?" Mam marveled, smiling without her teeth. She took them out of her pocket, remembering, and seemed to eat them in two bites. "Well, Lord bless this little new child. And let him have a loving world to live in."

Salty lingered to help her in to breakfast, dreading to be alone with Tom. Mam tied her cane to her waist with its shoestring and tapped slowly into the dining room. But without Jo, she didn't want to risk it. She followed him into the kitchen. Tom had left an empty coffee cup, and was gone.

Rose Ann waited until Hardy came from the bakery so they could eat together. Salty warmed the coffee and ham and biscuits and cooked them eggs. When he went into the dining room, they were sitting across the table from each other instead of side by side.

He thought they would be talking about the baby, but Hardy was saying, "The last time you visited that sophisticated sister of yours she talked you into bobbing your hair. I don't want you to go."

"Hardy, it's just a simple visit, for heaven's sake," Rose Ann said with a small anxious laugh. "Besides, we need a rest from each other — time to think. Just a few days."

"Forget it. I don't want you going. Even if we had the fare. She does your thinking for you when you're with her."

"But it's all right for *you* to tell me what to think?" Rose Ann felt Salty behind her and stiffened. "I've already written her I'm coming."

"Well, write her you've just changed your mind." Hardy pitched Salty a doughnut he had brought home in a scrap of waxed paper.

Rose Ann stood up. She braced herself to say something that seemed to surprise and frighten her. "I asked her to send me money for a ticket. When it comes, I'm going."

"Damn it, Rosie, I'll pay for what you do."

"Hardy, it's for both of us. Can't you see I'm trying to help?"

"God," he said. "Haven't you helped this marriage enough already?"

She left him sitting at his breakfast. Salty hovered behind him, not sure he was needed. The edges of Hardy's hair that had stuck out from under his bakery cap were dusty with flour. He looked older than yesterday. Salty took Rose Ann's plate to the kitchen and came back to wait again, nibbling his doughnut.

Finally Hardy said, "So I missed all the excitement." Salty nodded, wondering if Hardy was sorry Jo's baby was the special one. "Do you think New-Mama would let me see the little miracle?"

"She let me," Salty said.

All that afternoon Babe insisted Jo had to rest. Salty sat on the stairs to wait. When Babe finally came to say he could visit, he was asleep on the carpet. Everyone had eaten when he woke. Babe had saved him supper. Thankfully he ate alone and did his chores and went to bed.

But he lay wide awake on the bed where a new child had squeezed its way into the world. Slowly he went over the house in his mind, the way the last one up might go, checking the sleepers in their rooms. Mam snoring. Tom and Babe sliding like topsoil into the valley her weight made. Hardy and Rose Ann on the edges, not touching, until he rose to go to work. And Jo smiling in the dark as she listened to breathing that had never been before.

Then in his mind he came back to his room and saw the ugly, bony tangle of himself knotted in the hollow of the bed.

CHAPTER THIRTEEN

O N Saturday Babe allowed Salty to take Jo's breakfast up. Jo had the baby on her lap, holding his red, crimped-up legs while she got a diaper under his scrawny bottom.

"Phew," she laughed. "I'm nearly as helpless as Stinky here. How's he going to change the world, when I can't even change him?" She gave Salty the dirty diaper to put into an old chamber pot Babe had brought up from the basement. The baby had a wide band around his middle, as if he had broken in two and been mended.

"Don't he ever open his eyes?" They were clinched like Salty's when he couldn't bear to come awake.

"The world will get more interesting in a few days." She laughed. "For me too. All I want to do is eat and sleep and look at him."

Lovingly she handed the baby up to Salty. He clutched the blanket that sagged with warm weight and eased it into the basket. The baby bowed up with small, underwater last-gasps, testing the dry air with his octopus arms.

"Hardy came in last night," Jo said softly. "He looked at the baby so long. And he took his little foot in his hand, and said, 'I want one just like him.' "

"Did Rose Ann hear him say that?"

"No," she said. "I wish she had."

Salty went to the window. The owner of the Buick had fixed his flat and driven away.

"Is he going to change the world?" he asked.

"Oh, Salty. We all change the world, don't we, by taking up space in it a little while, and touching each other's lives? Painting houses? Buying bread?"

He was silent, knowing she was right, but disappointed. It didn't seem special enough, just to leave a faint thumbprint on life.

"I lie here thinking such strange things," Jo said. "His little neck. The back of his little trusting neck. I saw a picture once of a hanging-tree they used in the French Revolution, full of bodies. Men who were like him once, in their mothers' arms, and I began to cry like an idiot and pray for him, for when he's thirty and when he's old. Everything is so intense. As if I had two sets of nerves to feel the world with now, his and mine."

Salty watched the baby push and strain and snort, feeling something like her fear for his helplessness. What if he needed them and couldn't say, couldn't point to what hurt? Couldn't even live, if they walked out of that room?

"I feel as new as he is," she said, digging into her breakfast. "I feel so fierce. Confident enough to direct my own life, finally, that someone else has always directed for me."

"Are you going to tell your husband, like Tom was talking about?" He didn't want her to. He wanted to learn from her how to hold out against somebody. To close off everything but resistance.

She dabbed the crumbs on her tray painfully. "I have to, don't I?"

"No."

"I have to, Salty. This is his son. If I were out there, wondering where he was, if he'd been hurt — I'd want to be told."

"But you left him. Haven't you left him?" Suddenly he couldn't let her compromise. "He lied. He blinded people! What kind of a father is that? You're better off without him." He glared into the sheen of morning, feeling her push her tray away, feeling her eyes.

"I know all that," she said gently. "You're a loving person, Salty. Tell me something better than that. Help me know what to do."

Hate him, he said in his mind. Hate him. Show me how. He mashed his lips together. Across the street, Idalee surged out onto the Eversoles' porch on a wave of yells from inside and stood crying in the summer sun.

"I'm not loving," he said.

"Don't say that. What's wrong? Can you tell me?"

"No," he said.

They stared out at the morning. At last Jo drew the tray close again and ate.

At noon Mam wouldn't come to dinner. Salty finally got the reason out of her: while he was upstairs with Jo, Babe had bustled into the kitchen right in the middle of Mam's breakfast, and cleared away the dishes.

"But, Mam, you have to eat," he said.

"No. I can live off my dignity a long, long time," she told him.

He was sneaking her some late dinner when Babe came by. She hesitated, then made her pearly smile. "Could you help Tom again today? Saturday's the hardest, you know, everybody going home stops by, getting fixed up for that Sunday iced tea and red gelatin and peach ice cream."

"I don't think I was much help," he said, and eased past with a sandwich for Mam.

As he turned in the hall, he saw Idalee slithering upstairs

like a lizard. He dropped Mam's sandwich and grabbed her. She came tumbling down on him and they piled up in a rock slide at the landing.

"What do you think you're doing?" he demanded around her knee.

"Nothing." She sat up, arranging her face into round, loose-mouthed innocence. "I think I was lost."

"I think you're a snoop." He gave her a boost toward the door. "You stay out of houses unless you knock and people let you in. You understand?" He wondered what she had been crying about when he saw her from Jo's window. A bawling out, probably. Like he was giving her. He let his voice soften a little bit. "Who was you looking for?"

"You," she said. "Can you play?"

He drew himself up. "No. I'm too busy. And you're too little. Scram."

She backed off, poking her lower lip in offense. "What's the sandwich on the floor for?" She gave a hop and landed in the middle of it on her way out.

While he was cleaning the rug, Rose Ann came down the stairs in a little flower hat and white gloves. She carried a bag. It looked like that movie where the cowboy's girl packed up and left him. Hardy came behind her with his shirttail out, saying, "What's my schedule got to do with it?"

"Just that you work most of the night and sleep most of the day," she said. "I might as well be visiting her."

"We used to spend the night and half the day in bed and you never complained you needed a vacation."

She laid her white hand on the dark elbow of the stair rail, touching it in farewell. "That's all we were good at, wasn't it? That's really all we were good at together." She gazed up at him as though she had never seen him from that angle before.

"The least you can do is tell me how long you're going to stay."

"I don't know how long."

"Well, how long! How many days?"

"Hardy, it's a simple visit to my sister's. Girl talk. A rest. Let me have the time I need."

"Okay." He made a gesture, sweeping her out. "Sure. Salty, how about fetching the lady's bag to the train station?"

"I prefer to carry my own bag," she said.

"Okay." He stretched his face into a grin. "Trot along, then. Have fun. Give big sister a poke in the nose for me."

"I'm not going for fun," she said faintly.

"Well, try your damnedest, kiddo. Somebody ought to be getting some fun out of this."

"Hardy. I wouldn't have to go at all. If you could — if we could —" She took a little square of lace from her pocket and pressed it to her mouth. Foolishly, Salty braced to hear it trumpet the way Hardy's trick handkerchief had, so they could all burst out laughing.

"If I could arrange my life to suit you?" Hardy said. "Make money? Grow up? Settle down?"

"If you could just say 'Stay.'"

Salty stood up, alarmed by her wide-spaced words. Say it, he begged. You want to say it.

"If you could just tell me I'm a permanent part of your life, Hardy. Not something you'll walk away from like your jobs and your rented rooms when you want out."

Hardy's smile flickered like a candle that her breath had reached. "Walk away?" It steadied itself. "You made certain I can't do that, Rosie. God, couldn't you trust me to love you?"

She took the last step down and stood so close that Salty could see the light of the front door swimming in her eyes.

"Don't you think I know how you feel?" Hardy said. "Sure, it's hell for a little rich girl to scrape through life with a bum. Sure, I'm everything your family warned you I was. But Rosie, all marriages have growing pains. Ours could heal. If you could give me a little more time."

She was close enough to smell. She smelled like the powder on babies. They would smell the same way, she and the baby curled up like a bean inside her that she was carrying away.

"There never would have been enough time, Hardy."

They studied each other's faces. Kiss her goodby, Salty said. What if the train has a wreck? Kiss her goodby.

Rose Ann walked past Salty without seeing him. When she reached the edge of the porch the sun caught her like a thin piece of paper thrown into a fire. He watched as all her edges began to burn and she dwindled to grayness far down the sidewalk.

CHAPTER FOURTEEN

WHEN Babe and Tom got back from church, Salty and Hardy and Mam had Sunday dinner ready: hot dogs, fudge, chili, and butterscotch pudding. It almost took Babe's breath just to thank them. Mam faded away to her room with a weenie in her pocket.

Babe took off a hat ripe with cherries. "Remind me to tell Jo about the prayer chain my Bible class started for her."

Tom had a fat, big-city Sunday paper under his arm. He looked different in his black suit, with his Adam's apple hung on a collar too loose to fit. He slid out the funny papers and handed them to Salty. Salty took them stiffly, letting his mouth make a mumble that could be thanks. He backed himself away, trying to picture what a chain of prayers would be, each thought linking Jo to God. He wondered if anyone but Mam had ever prayed for him.

While Babe and Tom and Hardy were finishing in the dining room, he sneaked a tray to Mam. She was rocking steadily and had a mouthful of something harder than snuff.

"Where'd you get pecans?" he exclaimed. "I thought you was on a hunger strike."

"I just don't eat *her* food, in there," Mam said. "I have my own that I picked up in the yard." She tucked a nut under the rocker of her chair and smashed it with one tilt.

"But Mam, look at the floor — shells, and everything greasy."

"Oil's good for the floor," Mam said, scooping up a mess of shells and picking pecan bits out of it. "We used to sweep our floor with oiled sawdust." She smiled. "Your great-granddaddy was a great one for pecans." Salty closed his eyes. He knew what was coming. The story about the good overseer who let Alford and the work crew scrabble for pecans along the Trinity.

When he took Jo's tray up, she was nursing the baby. It didn't seem necessary to feel awkward when she looked so natural, so he grinned when she did and said, "Now you both can have your dinner."

"Chili?" she said, sniffing. "That's not Mrs. Buckley's idea of Sunday splendor."

"We surprised her," he said. "Hardy needed something to do, to pass the time."

She let him hold the baby while she ate. He sidled up and down, watching his feet like someone learning to dance, with the baby hung over his shoulder to belch. From the window he saw all the Eversoles still packed in their car, reading the funnies.

Jo said, "Have you thought about what we were saying yesterday morning?"

He shook his head. He couldn't think about anything or feel anything. It was strange, but his feelings were frozen. All he could think of — no, all he *wouldn't* think of — was the man who didn't want him for a son.

"Mr. Buckley asked me again what I was going to do," she said. "I told him I'd give him an answer. Tomorrow. Next day, for sure. I might be able to travel by then."

"Travel where?"

She shrugged. "I can't stay here forever, freeloading."

"What did you run away for, if you was just going back to him?" he asked stiffly.

"I didn't say I was."

"You're trying to get me to say it. Say forgive him. Be like it was." His voice climbed accusingly as if she were choosing between him and Kell Miller. He clamped his mouth. In the silence, the baby made the little gurgles and squirts and wheezes of living.

"It can't be like it was. I can't be like I was." Jo pressed her knuckles into her sloppy belly. "Kell can't either. Not if he's hunting, worried about me. Not even if he's back at work, just cold and angry. It's an awful thing, you know, Salty. To be bonded so closely to somebody, and then to be opposed. It must be the most terrible thing that can happen to people."

Salty shoved the baby into the basket, forgetting to support his head. It bobbed, carrying the baby's gaze past one object after another indifferently.

"Stay with us," he said. She had to. He needed her. Who else but Mam had ever told him he had goodness in him?

He took the tray back to the kitchen and helped Mam out to the front-porch rocker. With great care they divided the paper and studied the bright boxed lives of the Katzenjammer Kids and Skeezix and Jiggs and Maggie and Mutt and Jeff, too curious to think to laugh.

Tom, in his everyday clothes, was watering the flowers. Salty could see Babe at the parlor desk, staring into the account book. Hardy wandered out, polecat-lonesome, and took his turn with the funnies.

The Eversoles came parading across the street in dish towel cloaks. Idalee had made herself into Sir Walter Raleigh by tucking the hem of her skirt under the elastic of her bloomer legs. For enforcing order she was lugging the leg of an old brass bed with the castor still on it.

"Get on your knees for the queen over there, varmint," she said.

"Varlet," Hardy said. "You've got your movies mixed, if your lordship will forgive me."

She aimed her scepter at him. "Can Salty play?"

"I'm not sure." Hardy grinned down at Salty crunched behind the funnies. "You do still play, don't you?"

"Not that kind of stuff. That's for kids."

"What!" Hardy jerked him up and headed him into the hall. "Is Barrymore for kids? Was Valentino? Is ten thousand dollars a week for kids?" He steered Salty into the basement and opened a trunk.

Salty let out his breath. The trunk was full of costumes and wigs and things for acting. It was like a whole movie mashed together.

"Is this yours?" he gasped.

"My folks were both teachers — they loved theatricals. What the schools wouldn't furnish, they'd buy or make themselves." He pulled out a long length of plush with a split in the middle. "When they separated and cleared the house, I took the trunk. It's what I wanted to remember about them. The make-believe." When he dropped the cloth over Salty's head it fell to his knees in rich folds.

"Hey," Salty said, embarrassed. "It's a dress."

"Sire, nay! A royal tabard." Over it Hardy threw a cape with a glowing red lining, the most beautiful thing Salty had ever seen. It slid like red ice as he turned.

Hardy rummaged in a box of Babe's things. He placed an embroidery hoop on Salty's head.

"A simple circlet for everyday, sire. We don't wish to appear gaudy." From a little box in the tray of his trunk he took a short stick like chalk and marked Salty's face. Suddenly he dug down and brought out a real sword. He slid the hissing blade out, then sheathed it again. "Don't draw," he warned. "If you skewered an Eversole we'd both go to the rack."

Salty, still agape, was trundled upstairs again and right into Tom and Babe's bedroom, where a long-mirrored wardrobe stood. He didn't recognize himself. He had a mustache and beetling brows and wrinkles and sideburns. He spread his cape and laid his hand on the hilt of his sword. He looked like a king.

He gazed into Hardy's smiling face in the mirror, not sure which he admired most — the magical new person he had become, or Hardy's way of making magic.

When Hardy launched him out onto the porch, Mam gave a start. "Salty?" she asked, then reared back and clapped her hands. In the parlor Babe murmured, "My stars." Behind his regal visage Salty exploded with satisfaction.

Idalee's mouth dropped open. "Jeeters, that's the gnat's bristle. Whooee. That's the canary's jawbone." Without a moment's hesitation she handed him the scepter.

He wasn't quite sure what he was supposed to do, but the Eversoles caught up the corners of his cape and towed him into the street.

"Play like we all want to be knights," Idalee said. "You have to knight us." He looked uncertain, in a kingly way. "On the shoulder," she explained. "Tap."

He knighted everybody with the bed leg, whirling a lot to make his cape spread. He wished he had the nerve to knight Idalee right on the nose.

"Is that what you're going to wear for the parade?" she asked.

"What parade?" He wondered if her folks, looking out,

would recognize who she was playing with, under all the royal rigging.

"Fourth of July. I bet you could win. Everybody dresses up and the best ones get prizes. Real money. This isn't my costume. I'm going to be Clara Bow, with lip paint and silk stockings."

The second Eversole said, "Daddy won't let you."

"He won't know. On top I'm going to be a ghost. But underneath I'm going to be Clara Bow."

"Can just anybody go?" Salty asked. He could win, with a costume like this.

"Unless you're over sixteen. Which you can't be."

"Nearly," he said casually.

"Horsefeathers. Didn't I see you at school? You're just one grade ahead of me and I'm going on ten."

"I don't know if you saw me or not. I probably won't go to school no more, anyway. I'm too busy helping run this place." He whirled just enough to make his sword swing out and whack her shins.

"Hey, you stop that!" She gave him a slap that sent his embroidery-hoop crown rolling down the street.

He grabbed her hair and faced her toward it as it wobbled into the gutter. "Go get it," he commanded. He could taste blood inside his lip. "King's orders. Go pick it up."

"You go fly a kite," she answered, looking Chinese with her scalp stretched. She began to cackle. "Your mustache smeared onto your nose when I smacked you."

He propelled her down the street toward the crown, blazing with the certainty that he was ruining everything.

A hand caught him by the ear and jerked him off his feet. He squirmed around, nearly nose to nose with Mr. Eversole. "Remove your hands from my girl," Mr. Eversole said with a scowl that could wilt a tree.

Salty turned loose. "Yessir," he gulped. He could feel his beetle brows melting under popped-out perspiration. He tried to melt the rest of himself out of the gripping hands. Idalee peeped out from behind her father's ham-shaped arm, making a face that looked better than her real one.

Out of the corner of his eye, he saw Tom watering the bushes along the sidewalk instead of the flowers by the porch where he had been a minute ago. Tom sang out, "How's it going, Roscoe? How's your back?"

Mr. Eversole dropped Salty and lumbered around like a bombed tank. "Is this yours?" he bellowed, indicating the wilted king. "Keep him away from my kids!" He lumbered back, fanning his brood out of the street into their own yard.

Salty got his crown, wooden with humiliation. As he detoured around Tom toward the safe dimness of the Buckley Arms, Tom held out his hand. Salty's heart began to thud in confusion. Tom had seen it all and had rescued him and was smiling. He could see kindness in Tom's face, the understanding of an ally. Two days ago he would have leaped to match it with his own smile. Now he turned his head and hurried past.

Babe leaned out a window. "Salty, where on earth did you put the clothes last night when you brought them off the line?"

Every Eversole stopped in the street and looked around. Salty wondered if he could pretend he didn't hear.

"Salty," she yelled louder, "where did you —"

"In the sprinkle bag," he answered, as low as he could.

"Where?"

He could hear giggles. He lifted his head. "I sprinkled them and rolled them in the bag to iron tomorrow."

Little titters bounced like sparks. "Haw!" Mr. Eversole shouted, grabbing the two youngest under his arms like bags of flour. They all went laughing into their house. Only Idalee hesitated just a second in the doorway, looking back.

Tom studied Salty's blazing face. "So she's got you ironing?"

"Sort of. Easy stuff. Pillowcases and stuff."

"Don't they teach you English at school?" Tom asked wearily. "Sort of. Stuff. Don't you read, or anything?"

Salty watched the water run past his toes on the sidewalk. He could feel the windows of all the houses watching him like eyes.

"And don't you care whether that gander of yours has water or not? His crock was dry as a bone when I filled it."

Salty struggled with his mouth, swallowing his humbled pride. Regretfully, as if he had taken his thumb off a hose, he let himself go. "I know who you are," he said softly.

Tom glanced toward the porch. His teeth made a white, fenced smile like the ordinary response to an ordinary remark. "You'll know when I tell you," he said.

All the questions boiled up in Salty's throat. He could feel the embroidery hoop changing shape in his hands. "Didn't I mean anything to you?" he began, but as he said it, Tom bent, coughing, and dragged the hose away.

Hardy found him in Tolly's pen. He leaned patiently on the fence. Salty got up and followed him into the house, thinking Babe had sent for him to do the dishes. The kitchen was clean. Hardy led him down into the basement and opened his parents' trunk. "It's time to decide what you're wearing in the parade Thursday." He lifted things brightly. "You still want to be the Emperor of All-He-Surveys?"

Salty looked past him at the door of his room, where the most miraculous thing in the world had happened. "I don't want to be anything."

"Oh, come on," Hardy urged. He lifted out a frizzy orange wig. Then a big, black beard attached to wires that hooked over the ears. "How about if I go with you? Dressed alike. Funny hats."

"I told Tom."

"Oh, boy," Hardy said.

Salty stroked the orange wig. "He walked off. Like I hadn't said anything."

"I saw it," Hardy said. "What did you expect? Right out there in front of God and everybody?" He set a three-cornered hat on Salty's head. "We ought to get something straight," he said, trying each corner toward the front. "If you want to stay here, you can't do that again."

"I don't want to stay here."

"Where'd you rather go?"

He went hollow, not knowing.

"Back to the river?" Hardy asked. "To Kansas City with Jo? To visit Rosie's ritzy sister?"

Salty shook his head, knowing where he wanted to stay, no matter what his mouth said.

"Tell you what," Hardy said quickly. "Let's make little New-Mama feel better. All of us feel better. Let's put on a show. You and me. Skits. Songs. Yeager and McCaslin, the Kings of Comedy."

Costumes began to fly around Salty's head as Hardy heaved them out. He caught at them, remembering how lonesome Hardy was without Rose Ann. He took a letting-go breath and began to help. "I don't know how to do a show."

"Never to worry — you're in the hands of a master," Hardy said gratefully. "Come on, let's start before I have to go to work, right now while it's Sunday nap-time at the Buckley Arms."

They were trying to sneak into the parlor to pick some records when Babe caught them. "My stars," she whispered, and her chins dropped. Hardy and three pillows were stuffed into a long dress shaped like a pouter pigeon. Salty had on droopy tights and the black beard.

"Ah, an opera lover," Hardy whispered back. The three of them tiptoed to the Victrola and Hardy picked a record. He turned the volume as low as it would go. A soprano's voice rose up through the orchestra, coiling like silver wire. Hardy clamped his good and bad hands over his bolstered bosom and rose up too, pretending the voice came from him as he strained and gestured in exaggerated pantomime.

Babe collapsed in silent giggles. Salty gulped back a bray of admiration. When a tenor joined the lady in a duet, he awkwardly mimicked Hardy, throwing out his arms at the loud parts and clasping his hands in despair when the music went sad.

"Think an act like that will pull old Jo out of her heebie-jeebies?" Hardy asked Babe when they had pretended to bellow out the last triumphant notes.

She wiped her eyes, nodding, breathless from laughing. "Oh, I should be serious, with her up there so confused about her life, but you two idiots . . ." She seemed to sink gently, like the sad part of the song.

"Want to be in the show?" Hardy asked. "We need you."

"Me?" Babe flushed. "Oh, no. I'll change records for you. But I haven't done recitations in so long."

"You don't say," Hardy said, winking at Salty.

"Well, I *used* to say," Babe countered. They laughed. "I used to say 'Curfew Must Not Ring Tonight.' And 'Please Don't Sell My Father Rum.'"

"I remember," Hardy said. "You did 'Lips That Touch Liquor Must Never Touch Mine.'"

"Oh, my stars, yes. And 'Over the Hill to the Poorhouse.'"

"Do some for the show."

She studied her fanned fingers, as if they had surprised her by changing over the years without her noticing. "We used to do crazy things. Tom could play the banjo. And dance, soft-shoe like the vaudeville fellows. Not around his folks — they were too strict. But oh, he could shake a leg. What do you suppose happened to us?"

Behind his black beard Salty laid his tongue to the cut inside his lip, waiting for Hardy to answer her question, but Hardy was staring at a record. He put it on, and a faraway orchestra began to play "My Isle of Golden Dreams."

Babe heaved herself up out of her memories. "There's a box of old clothes and things under the stairs you two can use, if you want to."

Salty followed her into the storage closet. She opened a box. The smell of mothballs rushed out. Folded on top was something heavy, made of khaki-colored wool. A button glinted. Salty's heart began to tap like a twig at a window. "You mean I could wear that?"

"Tom's uniform?" She laughed in surprise. "It would swallow you!"

"I know," he said softly. "But, could I?" He felt a shiver ripple inside him as Babe hesitated.

"Oh, just any of this stuff," she said at last. "What else is it good for?"

CHAPTER FIFTEEN

Monday was washday. Hardy had come in at six from the bakery and was asleep, but Babe and Salty propped him against the wall long enough to strip off the old sheets and spread clean ones. While the wash was flapping dry in the sun, they picked beans to can, and set Mam to snapping on the back porch.

"You still don't feel good, do you?" Babe asked as Salty's silence melted her chatter. "I hope it's not typhoid, for goodness sake. Maybe a good dose of Epsom salts . . ."

He had been thinking how her eyes would stare when he told her.

"I'm fine," he said. He perked his face and tried to look recovered.

Hardy was grumpy that afternoon. They painted the front porch, each in his own silence, their faces bright with sweat and paint freckles.

Just as they were about to stop and rehearse their show, Babe sent Salty off to the ice dock to tell Tom to bring home an extra twenty-five pounds. Her twinkly smile made him think she had used up what she had making ice cream.

Tom merely nodded when he gave the message. While Tom loaded the last customer's truck, Salty waited with his back carefully turned on the narrow window of the engine room. Tom closed up and knocked the bugs out of his hair. They took the ice home on the back bumper of the car.

Jo's room was lighted up behind drawn shades. When they went into the kitchen with the ice, Babe yelled, "Surprise!" and led them upstairs.

Jo was sitting up in bed, lapped and double-lapped in one of Babe's bed jackets. Beside her, rocking a mile a minute, was Mam, with the baby in the crook of her arm. Hardy stood behind them, winding the Victrola he had brought up from the parlor. He started a record and a thin, happy voice began to sing, "When my baby smiles at me —"

"It's a naming party," Babe cried, shining like a full moon. An angel-food cake was about to drift off the bedside table. Something red sparkled in a pitcher, and the ice cream mellowed in the freezer, covered with towels.

"We can't call him swamp-bottom forever," Jo said.

Tom asked, "What do we do? All contribute a name so he'll be James George Phillip Henry Alexander, like some king?"

"Salty," Babe interrupted, "there's a book in the basement. On the bottom shelf, red, like a dictionary, with pages and pages of names. Turn on the light so you can see."

He sprinted after it, afraid he would miss something. There were dozens of dusty books and boxes on the shelf. He knelt and pulled on faded spines that might once have been red. A box toppled out and spilled gray cardboard rectangles over his knees. They were crazy. Each one had two identical pictures side by side on the front. He had heard about stereoscopes — these had to be pictures for them, and they were scary enough without having a third dimension.

They were about the war. In one, twin tanks reared up on the edges of jagged shell craters like monsters crawling out of the earth. In another, mangled bodies in soup-bowl helmets lay repeated in the mud. The back of his neck tingled. There were blasted trees and overturned trucks and dead horses like tipped-over statues with their legs bloated straight out. He tore his eyes away and stuffed the pictures back in the box.

A sheaf of photographs had wedged between his knees. The top one was of a soldier buttoned so snugly into his high-collared uniform that his strong neck bulged over it. He was looking into the distance, puzzled, as if it were a mirror. Salty put the packet back without looking at the others and stood up shakily. He had just seen Tom when he was well and brave, before the war had happened to him.

He almost started out without the book, but remembered. He spied it and hurried back up to the party. Babe was cutting the cake. A new voice was singing about finding a million-dollar baby in a five-and-ten-cent store. Jo winked at him. "Or in the bargain basement," she said as he handed her the book.

"Gad, this calls for fireworks," Hardy said with actor gestures. "Champagne. Twenty-one guns for Percival Cuthbert Mortmorency Miller."

"Aren't we getting more names than we have baby?" Jo laughed. She leafed through the book. "Doesn't anybody like just plain David? Or John?"

"What about your father's name?" Babe asked.

Salty cautiously looked at Tom. He had the same deep, puzzled eyes as the picture in the basement. The same jaw. A different mouth. As carefully not speaking as his momma's.

"Hey, look, it explains what each name means," Jo said. "Luther. Illustrious warrior. Morgan: a dweller on the sea. Joshua means Jehovah delivers."

"I thought the stork did the delivering," Hardy said.

Salty stifled a cackle of shyness. "What's my name mean?"

"Salty?" Jo said doubtfully. Her finger still underlined the last word she had read.

"Is Salty a name?" Babe asked.

"It means asked for," Tom said.

They all turned toward him in surprise. Babe put her thumb into a slice of cake. "*Salty?*"

"Saul," Tom said. "Saul means asked for."

Salty felt his hungry stomach flip. He pressed his fist over it. "How do you know my name's Saul?" His voice sounded far away, too high, like the mechanical voice going around and around on the phonograph.

Tom looked at Mam. She looked back at him, slowly rocking. "I asked," Tom said, holding her gaze with his. "I asked your great-grandmother what Salty stood for."

"Wouldn't it be wonderful," Jo said, finding it in the book, "if that was every child's middle name?" She made a mock-sad face. "My name was Ethel Joyce Shamburger. So I chopped off as much of it as I could and married young."

Tom sat on the window ledge because nothing else was left, and balanced cake on his knees so he could take the ice cream Babe was dishing up. "You could have been Joy," he said.

"Hey," she said softly. "I never thought of that."

Hardy started the Victrola again. A rich, sad voice began to sing, "Climb up on my knee, Sonny Boy —"

"Don't," Tom said.

Hardy took off the record and started another. "And now, ladies and gents, Yerkes' Jazarimba Orchestra presents —"

"Oh, yes, play 'Ain't We Got Fun,'" Babe exclaimed. "This is a *party*."

The baby began to cry.

"Wet as a frog," Mam said.

Babe handed him over to Jo. She diapered the baby on her

lap and asked, "Are you getting tired of holding him, Mam?"

"No," Mam said, reaching out her arms.

Hardy brought a paper sack from under the Victrola. He took it to Jo. "Here's a little something for your little something." He pulled a big teddy bear out by the leg.

"Oh, Hardy. How thoughtful! Thank you." She kissed the bear's wide plush nose, laughing. "Only maybe we should give the baby to the bear."

Salty pulled its twin out of the sack. "Is this one for the bean?"

"Oh, well," Hardy said, embarrassed. "While they were on sale — sure, for the bean." He held it against his chest, one-handed, kneading it with his big nervous fingers.

Babe put "Dardanella" on the phonograph and whirled Hardy and the bear around until his longing for Rose Ann strained into a smile. Tom said sourly, "Feeney must have had to advance you a week's salary for that."

"He did, indeedy," Hardy pulled a wad of bills from his pocket. "But not all for teddies. The rest for Tommy. Spent for rent. And continued next week."

Tom counted the bills and smoothed them into a thin brown wallet. "Fatherhood is improving you considerably. If this keeps up, we just might make it."

Salty bit intently into his third piece of cake.

"Here it is," Jo said all at once, bending over the book. "I like it. It's perfect." She leaned toward Mam and laid the back of her hand on the baby's temple. "Micah. Micah Miller."

"Does it mean something?" Salty asked.

"It means, 'Who is like God?'"

The music stopped. In the silence, the baby gurgled inside and smiled delightedly with a gas pain.

"I give up," Hardy said. "Who is?"

Jo closed the book over her hand, trying to decide. "Every

new child?" She laughed. "Then that means all of us, doesn't it?"

"Everybody?" Babe asked uneasily.

Hardy smiled and struck his preacher pose. "Saint and sinner alike, Sister Buckley. All God's creatures, burning with the spirit."

"I like it," Salty said.

"I'm tired," Mam said.

Babe took the baby from her. Salty and Hardy helped her down the stairs to her room. With the same care they carried down the Victrola, and the party was over.

Salty lay awake trying to remember everything. The baby had become a person right before their eyes. Micah. Someone who could be spoken to, written to, called back in a hundred years by the saying of his name.

It seemed strange that Kell Miller somewhere out there didn't know he had a son. Maybe Tom was right and he deserved to know. But maybe it didn't matter to him, any more than it had mattered to Tom.

Asked for. He had been asked for. His momma, glad like Jo, had wanted him.

But his momma would never have looked in a book. She wouldn't have known the meaning of a name unless someone had asked, This one? explaining it, and they had decided together, nodding, yes.

The word broke apart in his mind. He looked at it, as stricken as if he had dropped some familiar object that could never be repaired. Salty. Saul T. He could see his momma writing it out for Mam to read and re-form into a name she could call him. He could see his momma lay her pencil down.

Saul Thomas. Is that all you're ever going to give me? he asked Tom. The first letter of your name?

144

CHAPTER SIXTEEN

Tonight at 7:00
YEAGER and McCASLIN present
A SUPERCOLOSSAL LITTLE SHOW
for Your Entertainment in the Parlor

Hardy pinned the notice to the back of Salty's shirt as he started upstairs with Jo's dinner tray. Jo was watching Micah sleep in her lap, all lighted up with love. It was Tuesday, the day she had told Tom she would give him an answer.

"What did you decide?" Salty asked.

She shook her head. "Tomorrow. I'll tell him. I promise."

He turned around and let her read. She smiled.

She was there in the parlor when Hardy opened the sheets thumbtacked over the French doors for curtains and revealed the audience for their show. Babe sat by the phonograph. Mam held Micah. Jo had put on her dress and had color on her lips, but her face was as drawn as it had been the morning Micah came. She smiled hesitantly as Salty came forward to introduce the opening number.

Tom was late. They had eaten supper without him, in a

shell-colored twilight. Salty let his eyes sweep past the empty armchair, relieved.

Hardy came out in the black cape and pretended to be a bumbling magician. He whipped the cape off and held it in front of Salty to make him disappear. When he lowered it, Salty had slipped around behind him. Hardy, pleased with his magic, did other tricks while Salty crept at his back, holding his finger to his lips to warn the audience not to give him away.

Babe laughed so hard she bounced. Each time Hardy bent down to get a new prop, Salty whisked it out of sight. Finally, raving with confusion, Hardy turned and spied him. With leaps and collisions and near misses, he chased Salty around the parlor and out through the curtains, like the Keystone Kops.

Babe sobered herself and recited "Yellow-Haired Laddie" and "The Baby's Kiss" while they scrambled into their opera costumes. Hardy, frazzled from too much bakery and show business and not enough sleep, swore steadily as Salty shoved his broken arm into the tight-sleeved dress.

"They like us!" Salty hissed, astonished. "They laughed." They went back in and sang their duet with the record. Even Jo bent double, letting herself come undone with laughter. When they had made their final bow, Hardy fished a firecracker out of his pillow padding. Salty struck a match, and they froze, their hands almost touching.

"Not in my parlor!" Babe screamed. "The baby!"

They touched fuse and match. Flame sputtered in Hardy's hand, and with a bang, an explosion of little silvery stars fluttered down like snow over everybody. Micah jumped and went on sleeping.

"You *rascals!*" Babe gasped, catching stars in her outstretched hands.

Jo sat with her face lifted. Bits of silver drifted down upon her hair. "Oh, beautiful," she murmured.

Babe played records while they changed for another skit. She had lent them the bedroom to dress in, because it had the mirror. Slowly, with taut excitement, Salty buttoned himself into the itchy hotness of Tom's uniform and buckled the hard, curled puttees around his skinny legs. He tried to feel the bravery, and the fear.

They were going to play a record and sing along with it: "How ya gonna keep 'em down on the farm." He would be a hayseed soldier, and Hardy, as the city slicker, would try to sell him the Brooklyn Bridge.

It was a moment he had thought about since Sunday, when he had seen the khaki jacket folded in its box. He knew he had to put it on. He would have sneaked and done it, if Babe hadn't given permission. He knew he had to feel what it was like to be inside.

He placed himself before Babe's mirror. His shoulders almost filled the jacket. Gradually he gathered in air and bulged his neck, like the picture.

He had made a gun out of a broomstick and a broken board. He shouldered it.

The song started. He pranced out alone, singing like mad, and marched right into Tom coming from the kitchen in his dirty ice-house clothes.

The music pranced on without him. At the look on Tom's face he shriveled up inside the stiff armor of his uniform. "My Lord," Tom said.

Salty lurched backward, as if they were two cars meeting on a one-way road. Instinctively he leveled the gun.

Tom's amazed eyes raked him. He expected to feel the path of the gaze on his skin through the wool. "Get that thing out of my gut," Tom said. "You little scum."

He couldn't move. Horror fell like shrapnel all around him.

He felt Hardy drawing him backward through the sheet curtains toward the bedroom. Babe rushed past them toward Tom, her face as startled as his. "What did I do?" Salty implored, grabbing the newel post with shaking hands. "What did I do?"

Hardy shoved him into the bedroom and unbuttoned him. "Nothing. Hush. You came too close, that's all. Now, get out of this soldier suit and into your own clothes."

Salty stumbled into his overalls. His sweaty skin popped out in goose-bumps. "Is that all the show?"

"I think we just had the finale," Hardy said.

Salty groped through the kitchen and stood on the back porch, still shaking. He couldn't understand himself. He had never before needed to look inside somebody else, where the pain and reasons hid. Why couldn't he have left it alone and got on with the hating and hurting? What had he expected? Tom opening out his arms and saying, Hey, you look just like me?

Tolly had already tucked his head and gone to sleep. He wished he were asleep. So that what had happened could be a dream.

He went heavily around the side of the house and slid behind the scraggly arborvitae to look in at the parlor window. Babe was bustling out with the baby while Jo followed slowly. Hardy in his city-slicker clothes held Mam's arm as she crept toward her room. Tom sat with his hands between his knees, his face as still and blank as the dropped curtain. Babe's hand reached back inside the door and turned off the main light. Only a dim lamp glowed by the phonograph where the forgotten record turned.

On the other side of the arborvitae, something moved. Salty apprehensively lifted a branch. Idalee was at the other window, looking in as he was, her face flowery with lace-curtain shadows. He pushed through the shrubbery and caught her arms before he realized that she was taller than she ought to be. She came toppling silently down on him, clutching the stilts she had been standing on to see in.

"What's the idea?" he hissed. "You can't do that!"

"I'm just looking," she hissed back. "It's a show, ain't it?"

"Well, it's over. So go home."

"Why'd you stop?" she whispered. They stood up carefully. Tom was still sitting with his head bowed. Idalee stepped up on her stilts again. "You were really funny. You were funnier than Buster Keaton and Fatty Arbuckle put together."

"I was?" He remembered himself and turned his start of gratification into a shrug. "I'll probably be in movies like that. My friend and me, we might roller-skate out to Hollywood."

She was either too impressed or too skeptical to answer. Babe came back into the parlor. She stopped behind Tom and laid her hands on his shoulders. After a minute she lifted the record off and put on another one. A little jazz band began to grind out "Tea for Two." She smiled, nodding and clapping gently to the beat. She drew Tom to his feet. He took a hesitant step and shook his head.

"What are they doing?" Idalee whispered. "Why's she trying to cheer him up?" Salty gave her a poke.

Slowly Babe's smile faded. She went out again. Tom swayed after her like a flame following a beck of air. He looked at the phonograph, and his feet in their work shoes and white socks began to shuffle loyally to the song's beat. Idalee gave a snort that nearly blew her off her stilts again. "Is he trying to *dance?*"

Salty yanked her to the ground. "Listen, I said go home."

"But it's better here than at home," Idalee protested. "You're always having fun over here — can't I even watch?" She gathered her stilts to step up once more, but he held her arm.

"No." He was shaky again, mixed-up. He couldn't believe somebody was envying him this night. But she wasn't going to watch Tom dancing for Babe all alone with his elbows jutting out like grasshopper legs. "Get home," he whispered, wondering for the first time what it was like inside that house across the street.

"Not till you promise to let me see your duck."

"Tomorrow," he said, willing to promise anything.

"And let me have some of those little pretties that snowed down. Those silver things."

"I'll save the whole batch when I sweep. Now get home."

She got up on her stilts and hung to the windowsill as he tried to start her off. "Why's his mouth all stretched open like that?" she asked, looking in. Her voice dropped at something she had never seen before. "Why's he crying? Men don't know how to cry."

He pried her loose and chased her with a stilt, throwing it after her as she bounded across the street.

He couldn't go back to the window. The record had stopped. He sat against the foundation of the porch. He wished she hadn't seen it. He was glad he hadn't seen it. He wanted to hate Tom with no other feeling to mix him up. But he had already seen too much. The ghost of someone young and loving and uninjured, who had danced and made love to his momma and had died in the war.

CHAPTER SEVENTEEN

THE next morning, while Mam rocked Micah on the front porch, Jo walked slowly out upon the grass and lifted her face to the sun. Salty, painting on the upper porch, looked down at her, afraid she had decided.

It scared him. He wanted her to go on putting it off, day after day. Somehow, as long as she held off making any move, so could he.

Idalee rode up the sidewalk on her rickety bicycle and yelled at him, "When can I see your duck?"

"Gander," he yelled back. "I'm busy. Go home." He had the silver stars, mixed with a little rug lint, in an old envelope in his pocket, but he wasn't about to throw it down to her with everybody watching. She shoved off, pouting.

Hardy gave the railing a swipe and laid down his brush. "That's an idea. Let's take a rest and introduce Jo to Tollybosky the Terrible while she's up."

They went down to her. Hardy bowed with a flourish. She curtsied carefully and let them escort her back to the pen.

Tolly reached through the fence and dabbed at Jo's fingers. Finally he let her stroke his long neck and white taffeta back. Salty could have given him a medal for being so nice. She said, "You're beautiful, you big beautiful bird. You're a poem with feathers."

"He likes you," Salty said. He tried to guess by her face what she was going to tell Tom. "He'll get used to you real fast if you stay."

Through the wire she ran her fingers up and down Tolly's proud round front.

Hardy said, "Tom thinks you're hiding something. He thinks he's going to have to call the sheriff in on this, to get a decision out of you. Is he?"

She stroked Tolly's neck, making the quick breath that was like a laugh. "Izzy Wright?" Salty wanted to grab her hand and hold it still until she answered. "I thought all night. About three in the morning, all I wanted was to grab Micah and never stop running."

"Might be a little hard on Micah in a few years," Hardy said patiently. "Going to school in a new town every day."

She laughed, so close to crying that it was the same sound.

"You don't have to run," Salty burst out. "You can write him. You can tell him you don't want to be married with him anymore. Then you can live here and get a job and Mam and me can take care of Micah."

Jo and Hardy looked at each other. Jo said, "But, Salty. Micah belongs to his father as much as to me."

"No, he don't," he said, remembering the bloodstains on his bed.

"In a different way. What if knowing Micah made him different? What if he gave up this job and was a good father?"

Hardy said, "Very pretty, and God loves you for it, Sister Miller, but reforming a bad husband is a losing game."

She said, "Change places with him, Hardy. If I were Rose Ann, and you were in Kansas City waiting by a telephone . . ."

"It's not the same," he said, angry at being pulled into it. "Any kind of man can become a father in fifteen minutes. That's the easy part. The next fifteen years of loving a kid and providing for it and giving it an example to reach for — that's the hard part. He's not going to change, Jo. If you go back, you'll just be hoping in the face of reason."

"I know," she said steadily. "But if I can't hope for him, and love him, with all the ties we have, and all we've shared, who can? Who can forgive him, or care what becomes of him, if I don't?" She put her hand on Salty's knee as he knelt beside her, smoothing Tolly's wings. "Mam told me she almost killed her own son. Your grandfather. Because he hurt your mother, when she was a little girl. And yet, out of all that violence and sadness, you came, so loving, and it was worth it."

She lifted her hands and let Hardy pull her up. They all started down the alley, past the pungent cans of trash. She banged the lid of one of them.

"Hey. There's something grand about trusting like that, isn't there? Leaping ahead, even generations, and forcing good things to be?" She lifted her smiling face to the sun again.

"Don't go back," Salty said. If she went, she would take all that believing-in-goodness stuff with her. Even the good she saw in him wouldn't be there without her to believe it. "I was going to see what Micah did in the world. And take care of you."

Jo put her arms around him. He could feel her full, providing breasts against his bones. "You did take care of me. You have already." She smiled mistily, holding him back by the shoulders like a relative surprised at how he had grown.

He tried to think what it would be like never seeing her

153

again. Or worse than that. Seeing the backs of women and little boys on the street, and never being sure.

She said, "I know about you and Tom, Salty. I asked Hardy last night, after the show broke up that way, and we talked a long time. I wish you could have had Tom all these years. I wish he could have had you. You needed each other. I want Micah to know his father. I have to go back. I just have to risk it. Because more than anything I want Micah's father to know him."

Salty felt a chill fall like a shadow over him. It was as if she were offering Micah in place of all those blinded people, a little helpless love-gift that she believed had the power to change things.

Back at Tolly's pen a child screamed. Another voice yelled a string of words all bumpy from running and crying at the same time. They turned, startled. Salty charged back down the alley as if Tolly's infuriated honk had been a bugle.

Four Eversoles were in the pen. Tolly, with his wings unfurled like an avenging angel's, thrashed at them as they cowered and scattered. Idalee caught one wing tip. As Salty grabbed for the gate, Tolly broke free and swooped around to hack her across the arm with the hammer-hard hinge of his wing. Before she could open her mouth to shriek, he had nipped the seat of number-four Eversole and was heading for number two.

They stampeded past Salty as he opened the gate. Through his own gasps of breath he heard Idalee's bleating screams chopped off by the door of her house.

Babe came running from the back porch as Hardy and Jo rushed up. "Oh, my Lord, I thought somebody was killed!" She held her heart. "I won't have this. That goose is dangerous."

"But they were in his pen," Salty exclaimed. "They were bothering *him* — he didn't break into *their* house!"

"I won't have it," Babe said, ducking an invisible cannon the Eversoles had aimed at her. "They could sue us."

"But *they* were in his —"

"Oh, Hardy, run and get Tom. I don't know what to do."

Hardy took her fluttering hands. "Now, Babe, calm yourself. Let's just go over there and see what damage, if any, old Tolly the Terrible did, and take it from there." He started her off, gasping and patting her hair, across the street.

Jo heard the baby. She squeezed Salty's shoulder and hurried to the front porch. Salty sat down under Tolly's peach tree and closed his eyes. He could hear the rustle of feathers, as gentle as silk, as Tolly preened himself smooth again. "You've done it now, duck," he said, without looking.

"Whew," Tolly sighed, and grazed innocently on Salty's hair.

The moment Tom got in from work, Babe took him into the parlor and closed the door. Salty broke a plate fixing supper, afraid of what she might be telling him. Hardy came in and helped him glue the plate back together, saying, "Whoa, now, it's not that bad. Mama Eversole seemed like the kind who gives the kids a few bruises herself, on occasion."

"Babe's telling Tom," Salty said.

"I noticed," Hardy said, and hid the plate behind the stove to dry.

They heard the front screen. Tom was going across the street.

"Let's go scrape paint and let Babe break the dishes," Hardy said. He eased Salty out to the side of the house and set up the ladder. After a while they could hear pans banging.

Tom came back across the street and looked at them and went in.

It was bad. This time it was really bad. Salty felt the cramp of doom in his stomach. A voice inside the house said something almost loud enough to hear. He cringed and ran his knuckles over a nail. He went on scraping. But Hardy saw and sent him in to wash his hand and wrap it in a rag so he would stop bleeding on the wall.

Babe was setting the table and crying. Tom leaned on the table edge, nodding glumly at each muffled word she said. Salty stood in the hall, not sure that eavesdropping was really bad if it prepared a person for the fate that was about to overtake him. It was more like insurance. Suddenly a word sprang out that forced him to listen.

"That can!" Babe exploded. "That disgusting can. She knocks it over, Tom. Then she tries to wipe it up with anything she sees, a pillowcase —"

"All right," Tom said. "I know. You told me the other time it happened. But, Babe, if you can just hold out —"

"Tom!" she cried, slinging her tears away. "I've done all this before, don't you remember? While you were out with your little gun, winning the war, I was spooning oatmeal into that mother of yours and changing her sheets. You know what bedfast means, Tom. Four months, bedfast. And then, before I could learn to sleep through a whole night without her little bell tinkling, there you were, coughing your lungs out in that same bed."

"Babe —" he said.

"I'm tired, Tom. I'm tired!"

"I know that." He was pressing his arms over his stomach, gripping his elbows with both hands like some poisoned king in a movie. "All I'm asking —"

"She could live ten *years*, Tom. Are you going to carry the bedpan? You can decide about that crazy goose in five minutes, but I'm supposed to go on cleaning up after an old woman I don't know, wiping spit —"

"I'm not asking you to do it forever. We may have a buyer. He's coming tomorrow to look."

Salty bolted silently to the front porch and felt his way, dazed, around the side of the house.

"What did you wash with?" Hardy asked. "A dewdrop?"

Salty stared at the gummy blood on his hand, wondering what he'd forgotten. He went past Hardy and began to scrape again, drawing shivering breaths of dread. A few minutes later Tom got into the car and drove away.

When Babe rang the bell for supper, he said, "I don't think I'm hungry."

He waited until the kitchen was empty. Then he made up a little tray of sandwich fixings to take to Mam, to supplement her pecans. He sat curled in a cramp on her bed while she rocked and ate.

"At our house when I was a girl," she said, "we wasn't allowed on the beds in daytime. The menfolks stretched on the floor after noon meal, before they went back to the field. That was my mammy's rule. Now it seems strange." She bit a tomato the wrong way and it shot juice across her forehead. "Didn't seem strange then. Even when my pappy died on the floor."

Salty wiped the seeds and juice off with her big sugar-sack handkerchief. He wished he could walk from room to room in his mind the way she could, shutting doors on his troubles. He tried. "What'd he die of?"

"I don't recollect. I was little. Something quick, I hope, without a bed."

"Tolly's in trouble." He hadn't meant to worry her with

his problems, but it slipped out. He started a little sandwich from the bread and jars he had brought her.

Mam nodded. "Sounded like it."

He made a peanut-butter-and-mustard sandwich, but it tasted so awful that he made the next one with peanut butter and pickles.

"I'm in trouble, too," Mam said, trying the same combination in her sandwich. "She's mad at me. I forget to flush that contraption in the bathroom." He tried to pretend to laugh, but his tongue was stuck. "She's overly neat, it seems to me."

He gulped his peanut butter and cackled nervously in agreement.

"I don't want to get us throwed out," Mam said. "You sort of like the civilizing you're getting here, don't you — even when you resent it."

He could feel the house slipping between his fingers, like the other things he had lost. His momma. The river. He wanted to grab it, these rooms, even the pie they were starting on. He wanted to hang on until it all unknotted itself and came to rest. "Jo's leaving. She's going back to her husband."

"Is she?" Mam wiped tomato juice off the finger that bulged around her wedding band like a tree that had grown in a circle of iron. "She has to do what she thinks is right."

Pain had welled up in her eyes. "There'll be other babies to hold, Mam," he said, to stop it. "There'll be the bean."

"Oh, I've helt my share of babies," Mam said. "But she was nice."

"I know about Tom," he said. The pie fell off his fork. He stabbed it harder in a blur of desolation, giving her privacy to arrange her face. "Why didn't you ever tell me?"

She ate her way backward through her pie, crust first so that it was nothing but banana cream filling and meringue at the last bite. "I asked your momma in the hospital, February,

I asked her, 'Dovie, can't I tell him?' and she shook her head. So what could I do?"

"He's not going to tell Babe neither," he said. "Why is that? Is he ashamed of me?"

"Of hisself."

"That's stupid."

"Well, people set rules for theirselves. He broke one of his, is all."

He watched her close up the jars with the wrong lids and brush the crumbs into her cupped hand. "I'm going to tell her," he said.

Mam looked around, sad and tired, and finally put the crumbs in her pocket.

"Everything. Who I am. The house on the river he kept us in." His voice had ripples in it. "It's no good, living here. Always on the edge, not wanted. They're about to sell this place. But she's going to know, before we leave. I'm going to tell her."

Mam took his hand in her cold fingers that shook like the soft top of the pie he couldn't finish. "Baby," she said. "I know he's hurt you. I understand. But no, Salty. No. You don't want to do that."

"I want to!" He could feel her hands gripping, trying to press something into his flesh and bones that she couldn't find the right words for.

"Baby," she murmured, "he's just a man that happened to be your daddy. You've got a heavenly father that loves you and won't never forsake you. He's the one you want to honor and listen to —"

"God," he said, making it an oath and not what she meant. "Don't give me religion talk. I need help."

"I'm helping you," Mam said, but he had already grabbed the tray out from under her hands and was at the door.

CHAPTER EIGHTEEN

WICKWIRE didn't waste the Fourth of July sleeping. Fire-crackers started popping before sunup the next morning. When Salty went out front to listen, he discovered that Idalee had chalked public notices all over the sidewalk. SALTY DOES GIRL WORK, the first one said. SALTYS DUCK IS A MINNIS. I HATE DUM SALTY. There was a cross-eyed picture with its tongue hanging out.

He took the hose and washed them away.

It was a holiday for Tom. He got out the lawn mower again. They passed each other in the front yard without speaking.

Jo came downstairs for breakfast. But Hardy was asleep, and Mam wouldn't come. She shook her head, looking firmly past him, when he went to ask. He watched Tom spear toast and stir his coffee, wondering if Tom felt his thoughts as he stood behind him. Could he taste blackness, like soot, sifting down on his eggs?

Jo said, "Mr. Buckley, I wonder if you would do me a favor. I'm leaving today. I wonder —" She twisted her wedding ring. "I wonder if I could pawn this for enough to buy a train ticket."

Tom and Babe looked intently at her. "Honey, are you

sure?" Babe asked. Jo nodded lifting her grave eyes to Salty. "But, honey, it's so soon to travel."

Tom said, "There has to be a way we can manage a ticket without that."

"No. After all you've done, no. I want to do it this way." Jo turned the ring around and around. "If things are all right when I get there, my husband will redeem it. If things are not all right, I won't need it any longer."

Salty went into the kitchen and leaned against the sink, pushing burnt-toast scrapings down the drain.

Babe came bustling in. "Let's get last night's diapers washed. I'll iron them dry. And she'll need sandwiches for on the train. Hop, Salty."

Numbly he helped to gather what was needed. Babe gave Jo the laundry basket, packed with so many baby clothes and sandwiches that there was barely room for Micah. Tom backed out the car.

Salty put the basket in the back seat. When he returned, Jo was hugging Mam in the hall. "I'm going home, great-grammy."

Mam held her, nodding. "I won't see you no more," she murmured.

Jo turned blinking to Babe. "Thank you for everything."

"Did you tell Hardy?" Babe asked, handing her Micah.

"This morning when he came from the bakery." She looked at Salty. He braced himself. "Come to see me off on the train."

She put Micah into the basket. Salty got in beside it. Tom helped her into the front seat. They drove away.

At the pawn shop Jo slid the ring off her finger. Tom took it and went to the door. It was locked. Jo said, "Of course. The Fourth of July." They gazed into the dark interior through barred windows full of waiting things. Tom brought out his wallet and thumbed a thin sheaf of bills. He got back in the car.

"That was dumb. But I think we can make it."

"Will you pawn it tomorrow, then, and repay yourself?"

"Sure," Tom said. He drove to the main ice house and went into his boss's office. Salty could see the edge of his arm and shoulder through the window as he asked for an advance. His hand reached out. Jo rubbed her finger that was still pressed by an invisible ring.

They drove under the buntings on Main Street. The depot was decorated with exhausted flags and streamers. Tom went in with Jo to buy her ticket.

Salty put his finger against Micah's fist. Micah's earthworm fingers uncurled and curled again over his.

"You be happy," Salty said.

He got out when he saw them returning. They stood together, making sun-glare smiles, not knowing what to say. Far off, they heard the train at a crossing. Something inside Salty picked up its vibration and began to tremble. She was going back to do what she thought was right and he needed her.

They went nearer the tracks, where a little group of people surged. Tom set the basket on the bed of a freight wagon. Jo shaded Micah's eyes with an edge of diaper. Tom felt in his pocket. "You need a magazine," he said, and went inside.

Jo smiled at Salty. The train's nose poked out from behind the grain elevator like a weasel, and the rest of it followed, crouched and dark.

In front of all the people, Jo put her arms around him. He went as stiff as a railroad tie. Then he reached to hold her, too, with all his strength, so abruptly that their noses bumped in a sparkle of pain. Their chins found places to rest on each other's shoulders, and he could feel her soft belly against his, where the special child had been.

"You still don't have to go," he said.

She stepped back and held his hand over the corner of the freight wagon, with Micah between them like a picnic lunch for the holiday. The train growled and grew, shaking the air, and slowly creaked to a stop behind him, cutting off the light.

"Salty," she said gently, "people have to work out their lives in their own way. Wish me good things, the way I wish you."

She lifted Micah to her shoulder, just as she and Salty had stood fitted together in goodby. He could smell the ammonia stink of an already-wet diaper that would have to be washed next day in another place.

"I believe in you, Salty. I'll write you. And send pictures of Micah. I don't turn loose of people I love."

Tom came through the engine steam. People were boarding. He handed Micah's basket to the conductor.

Jo got on. Tom slapped at his pocket, yelling, "Wait, where do I send the pawn ticket?"

Jo said, "Keep it for me. I'll know where you are." She went in, and they saw her pass the windows, not looking out. You won't know when the house is sold, Salty wanted to tell her, but she turned one last time, smiling, and disappeared.

He watched until the train was gone, over the long soft hill like the curve of the earth, and not even the smoke was left. Tom stood beside the car until he came.

"We need to talk," Tom said.

"I want to walk home," Salty answered, and turned away.

"Salty —"

Somewhere a string of ladyfingers went off like the spurt of blood in his ears. He turned into an alley behind Main Street. He passed the ice dock and hurried through the rancid rendering-plant stench into the streets with houses. The train still trembled in him.

Tom's car was already parked in the driveway when he turned the corner at the far end of the block. A pickup truck was just pulling away from the house. The buyer, he thought. His steps slowed. Where would they go? They couldn't go. They couldn't scatter and leave it all unfinished. It would be like a body with a bullet in it, that couldn't ever heal. Give us time! he yelled silently at the pickup disappearing.

Hardy was standing on the porch, sleepy and rumpled. He anxiously checked Salty's eyes and said, "Let's get some costumes decided on. Can't let that parade take off without us."

He hurried Salty down to the basement. Babe yelled down, "Dinner's just going to be cold chicken and lemonade in the parlor, around the radio."

Hardy pulled out coats and funny hats and red wigs. He glued mustaches under their noses with spirit gum. "Don't gulp this down with your lemonade," he said. But he didn't laugh. He said, "Salty, I think I'd better tell you something —"

One of the basement windows darkened. Idalee was looking in. "Can I come down there?" she called.

Hardy hesitated, then unlatched the screen and caught her as she climbed through the window and dropped down. She carefully dusted overalls that were as mellow as Salty's.

"I thought you was going to be a ghost," he said. "With Clara Bow underneath."

"I can't go," Idalee said, licking a mosquito bite on her arm. Salty couldn't help but see the circle, black as a corroded dollar, where Tolly had hit her. He made a soft whistle through his teeth, hoping it would pass as an apology. She looked at the spot. "If you think that's something, you ought to see my behind. He split the hairbrush on me."

"You got a whipping?" It was the first good news he'd heard all day. "From your *daddy?* Why?"

She bent her fingers back, ticking off the reasons. "For bothering your duck. For writing bad things on the sidewalk. For saying he always whups me for what Purvis and Dixie and A.C. and Bootsie do."

"Sounds like you had it coming," Salty said, not as sure as he meant to be.

"Then he washed my rouge and lipstick off with carbolic soap, and I can't be in the parade." She shrugged off her woes and studied the pile of costumes enviously. "I could walk with you, though, and watch. And I'm sorry about your duck."

"Gander," he said, not quite sure what she meant.

Hardy started upstairs with the box of fireworks he had ordered.

"Sparkle sticks!" Idalee said. "Can I do a sparkle stick tonight?"

Salty looked at Hardy. Hardy shrugged. Salty mumbled, "Oh, well. Okay."

They went up to the kitchen. Salty piled their costumes on a chair. Hardy turned him toward the parlor. "Food," he said brightly. "Fabulous Fourth of July food!"

"I didn't feed Tolly yet," Salty said, and turned back. Babe and Tom both stopped in mid-step with trays full of dinner. The silence slowly filled Salty with apprehension. He went out on the porch.

Behind him Babe said, "Didn't you?" and Hardy answered, "I couldn't."

On the bottom step was the crock he had kept Tolly's water in. It was empty. A little curl of white down lay in the bottom. Salty's heart gave a kick. The rolled wire of Tolly's fence leaned against the wall of the house.

It felt like a joke, something he was doing in a show, on a

slowly tilting stage, while Babe and Tom and Hardy and Idalee watched raptly. He turned on Tom. "Where's Tollybosky?"

Babe took a step forward, like a soldier in line. "Now, Salty," she began, "this is something we had to do. The man came while you were walking home —"

Salty looked at Hardy's face hidden behind its mustache. "What's she talking about!"

Tom said, "It's just as well you weren't here. I sent your gander to a farm."

Salty stared. He felt the same pain as when the electricity had bolted through him. "No," he said.

Hardy took his shoulder. He slung Hardy's hand off and ran into the yard. There was no pen anymore. Only a square of sparse grass sown with little molted feathers like daisies.

Hardy came up behind him. "Salty, try not to —"

"No!" he yelled back at Tom on the steps beside Babe. "You can't do that. This is where he lived!"

"He belonged at the river," Tom said. "He'll be better off —"

"You brought him here where he had to stay penned," Babe said. "He can't live in town. He hurts people."

Tom said, "He'll be taken care of."

"You can't do that!" Salty bellowed.

"I already have. It was that pickup, leaving. When you came in."

He bolted around. He had seen Tolly carried away and hadn't known. "Where?" he demanded. "Where'd you send him?"

"I'm not telling you where," Tom said.

Idalee crept out and stood beside him. "I didn't do it. I wanted him to stay. I said he didn't hurt me."

His nose began to sting with tears. "Just shut up, will you!"

He ran around the house and stared down the street where the pickup had gone. With a cage in the back. A little white ghost inside, stumbling as the truck took corners.

Idalee followed. Hardy stopped behind her. "Salty, they're not trying to hurt you. This is a hard problem they're trying to solve."

Tom and Babe came through the house and stood on the front porch. "I made a bargain with you," he yelled up at them. "I was earning his keep — I have a say."

"Tom has the say around here," Babe informed him.

"But he's my gander. You can't give away something you don't own, damn it."

"Watch yourself," Babe said sharply, flushing. "While you work for us we're responsible for you."

"Babe," Tom begged.

Salty climbed level with her. "You don't own *me* neither, fat lady."

Babe drew back her hand and slapped him across the mouth. "Don't do that!" Tom ordered, catching her hand. "Damn it."

With dazed stateliness, Salty felt to see if his mustache was still attached.

Mam appeared inside the screen, her face a frightened blur. "Salty," she called, "what is it out there?"

"Get back to your room," Babe yelled through the screen.

A cold fury took him. "Don't you yell at her." He tried to push past Babe. "Mam, they gave Tolly away. That means we're next." He could see Mam's knotty hand pulling the shoestring to bring up her dropped cane.

"It's me," Mam said. "I'm the trouble."

"No! You're not," Salty cried. "We have a right to be here." He felt Tom take his arms from behind. He went rigid and looked into Babe's blazing face. He knew it was time. He knew he could do it. Like ice cracking he shoved his face into hers. "I got some things to tell you."

Instantly Tom yanked him off the porch, pinning his arms in a grip that snatched his breath. "No," Tom warned, "you don't have things to tell her."

"Salty." Hardy grabbed at him. "Don't do it."

"I'm going to," Salty gasped, and got the breath jerked out of him again.

"This is it, then." Tom hauled him around the side of the house. "Pack. Get your duds. You're leaving."

Salty turned in Tom's grasp and drove his knee into Tom's groin. Tom doubled up with a gush of sound, nursing the blow with his arms as Salty's fists battered his shoulders.

Hardy wrenched Salty away and towed him, bucking, into the kitchen. He pressed him to a wall. "Listen to me," he said. "Salty. Look at me. Calm down. Or I'll sock you."

The words made slits like razor cuts that he couldn't feel. Then he did. His rage began to coil slowly like water draining into a hole. He hung against the wall, saggy-kneed.

"Now, there's a parade starting out there, and we're going to be in it." Hardy released his grip and turned to dump their things into one of the funny hats.

Salty's hand, like a lever, reached out for Babe's rings lying on the cabinet and put them in his pocket. He and Mam would need money for a place to stay that night.

Hardy mashed the other hat on his head and led Salty out across the backyard. At the alley he turned him toward town.

The parade was gathering. A vacant lot was packed with floats and children and cars full of pretty girls in fluttering dresses. The mayor sat on the seat of the Wickwire fire truck with the driver. Hardy pressed Salty against another wall. He stayed, spent.

Across the street, in the park where the parade would end

after it had looped through town, Mr. Feeney, with his empty shirtsleeve folded up, fried doughnuts in a black caldron. Idalee appeared at Salty's elbow. He shivered.

"I've got money," she said, prissing on her bare toes because the sidewalk was hot. "I can buy a doughnut."

Salty slowly licked his bruised lip. His stomach jolted for the cold chicken and lemonade it had missed. Hardy felt in his pocket. "Salty? Want one?"

Salty shook his head. His fingers eased across the tiny lump that Babe's rings made in his own pocket.

"I meant we could share it," Idalee said.

He turned away.

Hardy put one of the red wigs over Salty's hair. He added the big pink ears and set the funny hat on Salty's head. "I can't do this," Salty said dimly.

"You can, damn it. You're going to march in every parade life gives you."

They waited in the narrow shade of the Wickwire Piggly-Wiggly. "I got to find Tolly," Salty said. Hardy stared at the sky. Across town, someone set off a blockbuster that made the dogs bark. "I got to. I won't leave without him."

At the park the flag lolled on its pole above Mr. Feeney's mountain of doughnuts. In the vacant lot, waiting, the horses for the Stockman's Association float swished and flicked patiently, dropping doughnut-hole dung.

Salty touched his pocket with rubbery fingers. The heat was melting all his muscles. He was different. He wasn't the person Jo had hugged goodby that morning.

"I don't want to go back there," he said. "Except just to get Mam." Hardy squinted off into the sun. "Only I don't know where we can stay tonight."

Someone with a whistle started the parade moving down

Deaf Smith Street. Hardy took Salty's arm and pushed him in behind a swarm of bicycles with crepe-paper wheels.

They paraded through streets with Alamo-hero names, Bowie and Crockett and Travis, under the swags of bunting. The blasts of the band shook Salty's chest.

As the trees of the park rose up ahead, the band fell into ragged formation beside a low reviewing stand. All the costumed children began to fall out of the parade there, to pass before the judges.

"Get over there," Hardy said. "Be the best." He gave Salty a little push toward the stand.

"I can't," Salty gasped, catching at a street lamp. "Stay with me. They won't know you're over sixteen."

"That's what I'm afraid of," Hardy said. He grabbed the end of a passing float, where Betsy Ross sat sewing away in a cotton-batting wig. "I'll see you at the other end when you come out with the prize." He rode off.

Salty took a deep breath and joined the line of contestants. A prize might pay for a place to spend the night.

Out of the corner of his eye he glimpsed Tom moving quickly through the crowd. All at once Tom pushed past the line of watchers into the street, and Salty saw that Idalee was tugging his sleeve and pointing. They went right past him, their faces intent, and hurried toward Hardy on the float. For a second he could see Hardy bending down toward Tom's jutting face, then the reviewing stand hid them as they turned into the park.

CHAPTER NINETEEN

SALTY ducked behind the reviewing stand, trying to catch sight of them through the bunting. Dimly he heard someone calling him back into line. For an instant he saw Tom and Idalee moving along beside the float.

Something had happened. Something was wrong. Salty gathered a breath and squeezed apprehensively through the crowd that was milling at the tail of the parade.

He saw Betsy Ross gazing off in astonishment, but Hardy was gone. Then he saw all of them, Hardy's red wig and great ears far ahead of Tom and Idalee. Tom had to break into a lope to grab Hardy's arm and stop him. Hardy jerked free and pushed on against the crowd, but this time Tom kept up with him, gesturing, trying to slow him down. Idalee trailed in their wake, holding Hardy's funny hat.

Salty shoved his way through to Idalee. "What happened?"

Tom turned in surprise. "This is personal. You and Idalee get on home."

"No," Salty answered. He had seen Hardy's face, with its mustache gone and a jaw clamped as hard as an anvil. He grabbed Idalee. "What is it?"

"Well, he jumped out of his car there where they blocked

the street for the parade and started walking real fast, so I did too."

Tom said, "Hardy, please. Slow down. Let's go sit in the car and talk this out."

"Quit following me," Hardy said. He swung suddenly into the Pictorium Theater, right past the usher, who threw out his hand and halted Tom.

"I'll get him," Tom said sharply. "Let me by." He pushed past, with Salty right behind him as the usher snatched Idalee by her overall straps.

Tom and Salty banged through the door of the men's room after Hardy. He was in a stall. Tom tried the door. It was fastened.

"Hardy. This is crazy."

"Just let me alone," Hardy said.

Salty waited dazedly, gulping disinfected air. He had to speak to Tom if he wanted to learn what was wrong. "What happened? Is somebody hurt?"

As if that nightmare scene over Tolly had never happened, Tom said, "Not at home, no." He looked around, but only the three of them were in the room. "Rose Ann's sister called on the telephone. She wants Hardy to come."

"Is Rose Ann sick?"

Tom's eyes swerved past his. "She hurt herself."

"Bad? Is the bean all right?"

"The what?" Tom asked. "Oh, the —" He stared at the stall door with the words scratched over it, as if one of them might explain something he needed to know.

In the stall Hardy hit the wall so hard it shivered. "Damn it, tell him."

"No," Tom said stiffly.

"You mean —" Salty went rigid. "The bean's dead?" He

172

didn't know how a baby could die, safe like that, or how anybody could tell, with it so little. "Are you sure?"

"God," Hardy said in the stall, and they saw the wall quiver again, as his fist slammed against it, and heard his breath shaking.

"Hardy," Tom said, "her sister could've jumped to conclusions. It could have been accidental."

They listened to his breathing.

"Hardy, if Rose Ann did it, you know she thought she had good reason." Tom wiped his face. "To give you time. Something. She's gentle, Hardy. She had to think it was what you wanted."

The usher pushed in, his hair knocked out of place by his tussle with Idalee. "Listen, mister, you've got to have tickets — all of you — or I'll call the manager."

"Get out of here," Tom said. "We'll come when we can."

"Now," the usher said.

"You're about to get your head shampooed in the next stall," Tom said, starting for him. The usher reversed, and raked the door shut behind him.

"What did she do?" Salty asked. "What did Rose Ann —"

"I wish to hell you'd go home," Tom said. Salty braced himself against the wall. He wasn't leaving Hardy. And he didn't have a home. Tom sighed and tried Hardy's door. "Hardy, give her a chance. Try to think what it took to do that. She needs to know you understand."

"I don't understand," Hardy said.

"Hardy, she's in a hospital. Don't you know what that kind of infection can mean? She needs assurance from you. Something. Now."

"What, for God's sake?" Hardy's breath got louder, grinding like a machine. "I was going to love him. Didn't she know that? Couldn't she trust me to find a way to love him?"

173

Tom turned away tiredly, and for a second, in the mirror, his eyes and Salty's met.

A new face appeared behind him, jowly and firmly set.

"Hardy," Tom said. "The manager's here."

Slowly the door of the stall opened. Hardy came out, holding the red wig and celluloid ears in his good hand. His real face looked strange and out of shape. He walked behind Tom out of the Pictorium and down the block. Tom in his hurry had swung into an alley to park. Idalee was standing by the car. Salty eased past her and got into the back seat.

Tom leaned on the fender. The car was nosed against a brick incinerator. People rushing to catch the parade had parked beside and behind it. They were blocked.

Hardy got in and wiped his face with the cloth Tom used to dust the seats. He bent over his knees like someone sick. Idalee backed regretfully out of the alley and turned toward home.

"You could call from the drugstore," Tom said in at Hardy's window. "She needs an answer, Hardy."

"I don't have an answer." Hardy took the thin little flask out of his hip pocket and looked at it a long time. Slowly he took a drink.

Tom sighed and slid in under the steering wheel to get out of the sun that was shattering itself against the blank walls. "She needs *you*, Hardy. She's your wife. Don't make her beg."

In the silence a wasp came in. With its long legs dangling, it looked like a child on his stomach in a tire swing. It walked on the windshield, examining the strange invisible barrier that kept it from the sky.

Tom shook his head. "Nobody should have to beg," he said, and gave up.

They watched the wasp climb. It said "Hmm," with a little bluster of hope, and walked on. Salty took off his wig and smoothed it. Slowly he uprooted his mustache and ran his tongue over the smudge of spirit gum.

He didn't understand any of this. He didn't see how Rose Ann could think killing the bean would make Hardy love her again.

But he guessed that three hours ago he had tried to kill the trust Tom and Babe had made with their love in all those years of being married, because he wanted Tom to love him. That didn't make sense either.

Hardy passed his flask to Tom. Tom glanced through the rearview mirror and took a nip. "What is this? Fuel oil?" Salty knew, by his voice, that they weren't going to talk about what happened anymore.

"Coon Hollow," Hardy said. "Don't expect White Satin for a buck a quart."

"I'm not much of a drinker," Tom said softly. "I'm a buttermilk man."

"It's your kind that gives Prohibition a bad name." Hardy stared at the blanched walls, holding the flask uncapped.

"My father was a minister," Tom said. "This isn't the spirit he believed in."

Up at the end of the alley, bits of the parade went by. Cars with streamers. A drifting balloon. The fire truck, going back to duty.

"I didn't fulfill his expectations," Tom said carefully, as Hardy's Coon Hollow collided with his empty stomach. "I had my own expectations. When I was a boy, my grandfather was mayor of Wickwire. I thought I'd be mayor, too, someday. I thought all that respect and honor came handed-down, like being king."

Hardy said, "You earned your share."

"No," Tom said, and held out his hand again for the flask. "I just kept rules. I just kept my father's rules. Even after he was dead." Salty watched his head tilt as he drank. His hair had been combed a certain way so long, it didn't have that little whorl that children's hair had. "I had meant to die too. Properly, in the war. But I couldn't. I had meant to be at least as faithful to my wife as he had been to God."

Fireworks went off. Da-go Bombs. Torpedoes. Deep, echoing bursts of celebration.

"But I wasn't," Tom said. "And then I knew that my life, with Salty in it, was going to be a long lie." He cupped his hand on the windshield. Warily the wasp greeted it and turned away and came again. It stepped upon his finger and walked into the field of hairs on the back of his hand. Tom moved his hand to the side window and the wasp leaped into the sun. "I knew it was going to be like one of those dark hospitals again. With no chance of ever healing."

"Tom, he's not an affliction. He's a boy."

"I couldn't let him be a boy. I would have owed a boy an education and discipline and values and a name. A chance at me."

Hardy said, "Still, don't you know I'd trade places with you in a minute?"

"I kept thinking. In the theater, there," Tom said softly. "When I was trying to make you see. Rose Ann. Why she had made that awful choice. I kept thinking. How different. How different, if Dovie had done that."

The floats were leaving. Washington's boat, on a cardboard Potomac, drifted past the end of the alley, empty. Don't you know I'm back here? Salty wondered. Don't you remember it's me you're talking about?

Hardy offered the flask. Tom shook his head. "Too much already."

"Not enough, yet," Hardy said, and drank.

"I kept thinking," Tom said. "When someone you care

about dies and you can't break down, you can't grieve, because of someone else. Like drowning. Slowly. Months. You'll know."

Hardy nodded.

Salty could feel them moving off through the heat toward their separate griefs. Tom to the funeral he hadn't gone to because he loved Babe, and Hardy to Rose Ann, who had thought he didn't want to be a father.

"So I never even grieved properly," Tom said. "Till now. Never did anything properly. Saw him once. When he was five years old."

Hardy turned around in the front seat and looked at Salty's hands stroking the curly wool feathers of the wig. "Do you want him to hear this, Tom?"

"I want to tell it," Tom said. "It's his, if he wants to hear it."

Hardy turned back. They all faced the incinerator. It looked like a rock their boat had foundered on. A little gray ash like spray blew from it.

"She was so simple," Tom said. "No, I don't mean —" He wiped his eyes. "Oh, Lord, so beautifully simple. She came back into that house and nursed me and loved Babe and smiled in that perfect silence and never asked anything of anybody."

In his longing mind, Salty asked, Can't you say you sat beside my bed because I might die and it mattered to you?

"Do you understand the way we were?" Tom said. "I never touched her again. We worked in that house together. In that silence. The years went by, and she didn't ask for a single thing. And I didn't give a single thing."

Salty leaned his head out and breathed the ashy air. Someone from a float turned into the alley. Miss Liberty. Carrying the torch gently in the crook of her arm. He didn't want to look at Tom's shoulders bent small as if all that spilled-out emotion was what had given them their shape. The emptied part of Tom left an aching space in him too. Like everything did, he guessed, that ever got born into the world.

"Lord," Tom said softly. "Why do we have rules for loving? For *loving*, of all things?"

Miss Liberty got into the car parked beside them and drove away. Salty put himself straight in the back seat. They could go now. He felt along the seat where Tolly had left the little gray dropping, but it was gone. Us next. Pack your duds. You're leaving.

Hardy said, "Tom. Don't you think Babe knows?"

"No."

"I don't see how a woman could live with a man and not know something that important.'

"She can." Tom started the engine. "A woman lived with you," he said. "And thought you were telling her to put your world back the way you liked it."

A blockbuster went off in the street behind them. Its breath shuddered against the alley walls. Tom inched back and forth until he could ease the car into the vacant spot and pull out.

Hardy leaned forward over his knees. Salty could see the design of the seat cover in the wet, dark back of his shirt. "Wait," Hardy said. Tom stopped. Hardy got out and held to the incinerator. They listened to his retching. Tom handed Salty the dust rag. Salty got out and waited until Hardy gathered himself up, cement-colored, and smiled at him. They got back in and turned out into the street.

"Let me off at the train station," Hardy said.

Tom turned into a street that followed the tracks. "Won't you need some clothes?"

"I don't know what I'll need," Hardy said unsteadily.

"Time. Clean underwear. Grace. Twenty feet of Babe's prayer chain."

Tom pulled up before the stone depot, the way he had that morning. He stretched one leg and brought everything from the bottom of his pocket. Without counting it he said, "If that won't do it, you can take the car."

Hardy counted the bills and change. "It's enough, Tom. Thanks." He got out, looking the way he looked the first time he got up on a roof after his fall. He leaned back in and took Tom's reaching hand.

"Tell Rose Ann we love her," Tom said.

Hardy nodded. He leaned in at the back door and gave Salty's arm a little punch.

"Will you be back?" Salty asked, afraid.

Hardy looked past his eyes to the wigs and bits of costumes. "Put all that back in the old magic trunk. Righto? For next time."

"We didn't do the fireworks," Salty said, to hold him.

"No. But we by golly did everything else today." He put on his actor smile and turned away.

Tom started home. The banded shade and sun of late afternoon rode up over the front of the car and down the back to the street again, dazzling Salty's eyes.

A car was parked in front of the house. Salty could tell, by the way Tom's glance darted past it to the front door, that it belonged to the man who might buy the Buckley Arms.

Tom stopped under the trees of the driveway and rubbed his forehead. He said, "Salty, I was wrong. In the way I handled the problem with your gander. I should have told you. Had it out with you. Beforehand. I didn't give you credit. I think you could have made the right decision yourself. If I had made the right beginning."

He didn't know what to answer. Or even if an answer was possible. He moved his mouth to see if it worked.

"We both said things in anger," Tom said, half turning toward the back seat, but looking instead at the porch, where Babe stood beside a man. "I don't want you to leave. I didn't mean what I said. You pushed me to say it, just like I pushed you to start to tell Babe. Can't we keep the bargain? It's a bad bargain. But can't we?"

Salty licked his lip. Too much had happened. His feelings were like hot street-tar that he couldn't move in.

Babe started down the porch steps. The sun struck her anxious face lifted in a question toward Tom. He got out and went to her. They climbed up to the man waiting in the stippled vine shadows. Salty curled tightly in the corner of the car. He knew he had to get out. He had to go on. Like Hardy. Like Jo.

He was startled to see the man go down the steps and get into his car. Tom was listening as Babe gestured in one direction and then another. Tom came down the steps, nodding. She followed him into the yard, and watched the man drive away. Just the instant before she raised her hand to shade her eyes, Salty saw that she was crying.

Tom opened the back door of the car. "Get up front," he told Salty. He backed out into the street.

"What —" Salty tried to ask.

"A little while after you left for the parade, your Mam went out into the yard. We thought she wanted to walk around a little."

"What do you mean. Where'd she go?"

"That's just it. When Rose Ann's sister called, and all that, nobody remembered —"

"You mean she's lost? She didn't come back?"

"Babe sent the Eversoles looking all around, and she went up and down the block, asking. But —"

Salty gazed out at all the possible streets in the long shadows. "Was she sure Mam didn't go back in and go to sleep in some odd place or something?" His muscles began to ripple with worry-shivers.

"She combed the whole house and yard. Mam's gone. Now think. Where?"

"To the river," Salty said. He saw her face, as she stepped back from Jo that morning. *I won't see you no more.*

"Oh, Lord," Tom said. "She can't do that. It's been plowed. The house is gone. Everything."

He cornered so fast they slid in the seat.

"She wouldn't try to walk," Tom said.

"She'd try to get somebody to take her by. We used to, times when she had to go into town. We got rides."

They roared out past the last houses, trying to overtake the tape of road unrolling ahead of them. Salty's eyes raked every crossing where she might have wandered by mistake or been let out by someone turning off.

"She didn't want to be no trouble," he said in despair.

They passed the spot where Tom had flicked the little paper marble of his momma's note into the roadside grass. "I'm sorry," Tom said. "We'll find her. We will."

Salty smashed his hands between his knees. He had to find her. She had never once, when he was little, let him get lost.

They jolted along the wheatfield. The wheat had been cut. The stubble looked like the prickled hair of a scared animal. Tom stopped the car. Salty sat stunned. The house had been trucked away. Or bulldozed and burned. The hard-packed ground where home had stood was a plowed field.

Salty got out and darted as illogically as an ant from one high spot to another that might give him a view. He thought how she had fallen that time in the yard and how small she would be in all that wild space if it had happened again.

When his breath was gone he sat down, clutching his chest like a bundle saved from a shipwreck. Gnats found his face and danced and sang as he panted.

Tom stumbled off across the plowed field. He called. The sound bounded back and forth along the banks, startling the settled birds.

What would she do? If she had seen the field where their house had been? Just sit down? Cry? Die?

Tom yelled, "Salty. I see some tracks."

He raced to look. "No," he said. "They're some kid's tracks. Wide apart." He let out his breath in disappointment.

Tom thrashed through a shallow thread of the river and climbed a sand hummock to look around. Then he crackled through thistles to the water's edge, calling and coughing.

"Let me do the hollering," Salty said.

Tom turned to look at him and lumbered into a slough up to his knees. Without thinking, Salty took a step toward him in regret. Tom pulled himself out onto dry land, holding his groin where Salty had kneed him, and went on, limping a little in his mud puttees.

"She's not here," Salty said after him. "She just didn't come this far."

Tom looked around. The wind had sunk to twilight stillness. He swatted something on his neck. "What if she did?"

As if he were being stretched in a rushing crack-the-whip line, Salty held his breath, queasy with doubt. He let it out. "You hunt in the field again. I'll hunt down by the spring barrel. Then we'll go. All right?"

Tom nodded and climbed up the broken shelves of the riverbank.

Salty pushed through grapevine tangles and ran across the

sandhills, crouching to be able to see any movement against the smoky blue last light of the sky. What if they left, and she was still out there somewhere? What if they stayed, hunting, and she was on some other road in the dimness, walking out of his life with little turtle steps?

He fell over the wires of a sagging fence and clawed into the musty earth. He rested, gasping, scraping mosquitoes off his arms. She had prayed for him so much, and he didn't know what to say for her. He got up and ran again, through the cool changing layers of air. He almost ran past the barrel. He stopped and called and waited. Only his breath broke the stillness. The gentle smell of rich life and rot hung above the spring.

He lunged up the trail into the level field. He could see the car. He could see Tom walking toward it with Mam.

Even in the dusk he could tell that Tom nearly carried her. She wasn't walking right. He bolted toward them across the clods and took her hand. Her weight sagged against him.

"Mam?" he asked. "Mam?"

"Easy," Tom said. He was holding her cane.

Salty could hear dark, heavy breath coming from her. Her fingers, that had always clamped his in welcome, made shaky twists like a long, unknown word in sign language.

CHAPTER TWENTY

Salty went cold. "Mam. What is it?" He could feel the change in her, the strangeness.

"The front seat," Tom said. "Between us."

They put her inside, slowly coaxing, directing her hands. Salty got in beside her.

"Salty," Tom said carefully, "I think she's had a little stroke or something. She doesn't quite know what's going on."

"What's a stroke? Sick? Don't she need a doctor?" He took her hand that was still speaking its silent word. It closed on his in the old reassuring way. "She knows me. Don't she? You know me, Mam. We're going home."

He began to shake, thinking how close they had come to leaving her out there.

"Getting dark, finally," Mam said in a quick slurred voice.

He gulped in relief. "Sure it is. It's getting dark finally — that's why we're leaving." He unreeled words to keep a connection between them. But she silently turned away.

Tom started the car. "I'll get her home as fast as I can. Reassure her. Let her rest."

He made a loop through the stubble that tilted them out of balance. Salty braced against Mam's sliding weight. She gasped a musty breath. He held her hand, so tightly that she had to know him and come back and be well.

"She was standing at the edge of the field," Tom said. "In that shin oak. Like just one more tree."

Salty tested his mouth carefully. "Thank you."

They bumped into the real road. Mam sighed and seemed to sleep with her head cocked against the back of the seat. Then she took a fresh grip on Salty's hands and looked around. "What is it?" she asked. "What?"

"We're going home," he said gently. "Nice bed. Nice rest. You're not lost no more."

She nodded, and slept against his shoulder, holding his hands so tightly that he let the tears slide down and drop from his chin without wiping them.

"Why'd she do this?" he whispered. "Didn't she know I'd take care of her, like she did me?"

"Salty. That's not a promise you can keep," Tom said wearily. "You've got your own life to lead."

He hunted for the sound of her breath under the car's roar, thinking what a wonder it was, the engine that had run in her so long without ever stopping to rest.

"Salty, you're going to have to be realistic. She may get to the point where she's like a baby. Where she doesn't even know who you are anymore."

"I'll know who she is," Salty said. He felt hollow. He knew he couldn't do it alone. "Somebody that loves her has to take care of her." But he knew somebody else would have to do something even finer than that. Help her without owing it to her. Without the love.

They could see thunderheads still lighted over town, the white, silent explosion of the biggest firecracker ever made.

"I want you to understand," Tom said with effort, "that

she can have a home. I want you to help her know that. Explain. She doesn't ever have to do this."

"What about that man?" Salty asked. "That was there when we come up?"

"I told him no," Tom said. "I said we changed our mind about selling."

Salty felt his heart trip with hope and thankfulness. But he thought of Babe who had changed her life around because he had appeared and said, Here we are. "You don't have to."

"Yes," Tom said. "I do." He glanced at Mam's tilted face, and Salty knew he was thinking of the ones who had cared for him, and the ones who would have to again someday.

"And Tolly?" Salty asked.

Far up ahead, at some farmhouse, a Roman candle erupted. Blue, red, green, the balls of color arched and dropped away. "No," Tom said. "The world doesn't work that way. You and Mam. Not Tolly."

"Can't I ever see him?"

"Someday. You can visit him. Not yet."

Salty gripped his jaw to keep the shivers from shaking his voice. "But he won't understand. He'll think I sent him off and don't love him."

"Geese aren't people," Tom said.

"They've got feelings," Salty said. "He loves me."

"Then he'll have to go on loving you on faith. Like people do when they can't tell each other."

A car came toward them. Salty watched its headlights lift Tom's face out of the dark a moment, and let it drop. "Like us?" he asked.

"Yes," Tom said.

Ahead of them, in town, someone who couldn't wait set off a rocket. Its ashes of light dropped like the silver stars that had fallen on Jo's hair. Salty doubled his arms over the spot that wrenched and ached for his lost things.

"Do you love me?" he asked Tom.

"Yes. You know I do."

"But you love Babe more."

"I loved her first." Tom looked out at the shadows of Mount Zion as they passed, and straight ahead again. "I've shared my life with her. I owe her more. I promised to honor her."

"But you didn't."

"So I make up for it now," Tom said.

They drove in silence through the edge of town and into the busy streets where the firecrackers popped. Smoke bombs billowed and rose like magicians' tricks to reveal laughing boys with wands of punk.

They turned off Main Street toward the Buckley Arms. Tom drove as close to the front door as he could, and they helped Mam over the grass and up the steps, straining like the wounded soldiers in Tom's stereoscope pictures.

Babe opened the screen. "Oh, no," she murmured. "Oh, Tom." She switched on the light in Mam's room ahead of them and turned down the bedspread. They set Mam on the edge of the bed. Salty tried to put her cane into her hand, but she only looked at it, puzzled.

"Water," she whispered. "For." A sound trailed off. Salty spurted out to bring it from the kitchen. But she was curled on her side in bed when he got back, sinking into sleep. "Scrabbling. For. While he watched."

"Pecans," Salty said. "Down on the Trinity."

"Alford," she whispered. She slept. He looked at her face. He had thought hate kept her remembering that time, but he could see by her smile that it was the overseer she couldn't

187

lay to rest. That flash of goodness in the badness of those days was what she was still pondering.

Tom motioned him out. Babe took off Mam's shoes and covered her with the bedspread. She followed them, switching off the light.

"Is she all right?" Salty asked.

"She may be fine in the morning," Tom said. "Waking up here, where you are, and her things —" He stopped, and looked at Babe.

Her face sagged, tired from all the searching she had done.

"She's tough," Tom went on. "These things heal sometimes. But not indefinitely, Salty."

He nodded. He knew what Tom was trying to say. She wouldn't live forever, nobody could. And after that, there would be no more Alford either, or pecan grove, or good overseer, except in him.

"You better sleep in her room tonight," Tom said. "In case she needs anything."

Babe said, "A boy can't wake up like that. I'll do it."

Tom gave her a steady look. "Just the same, Salty had better move up here to the little room next to hers. I mean, permanent. That way he and I'll both be handy to help you."

Babe looked past Salty, nodding. He wondered if the words I'm sorry would jerk out of her if their eyes met. Suddenly he remembered something. He dug into his pocket and held out her rings. She drew back as if they crawled.

Tom took them and slowly put them on her fingers, shaky-handed like the young men in love-story movies. He put his arms around her and laid his mouth on hers in a hard long kiss that went back past everything to the way they had started and had meant to be.

Salty turned away. As he reached the door, Babe said

softly, "Are you hungry?" He looked around to see who she meant, and she was looking at him.

"Yes ma'm," he said.

She smiled. "I'll put things out."

Salty went on through the hall to the front porch. He lifted his face to the dark night breeze from somewhere off a storm, full of all it had passed and lifted: field dust, flower scent, the breath of sleeping people.

His toe bumped the box of fireworks someone had put by the door. He bent down. The matches were still there, and the punk sticks he and Hardy would have touched off magic with. Something white moved in the swing.

"Ready?" Idalee said.

He was too spent to know what she was asking.

"We didn't do the fireworks yet." Her round face tilted hopefully in the dark.

"Hardy's not here no more," he said.

"Well, we are."

He drew a patient breath and picked up the box. They went around the house, trying to find an open spot. The trees lapped overhead. Salty stopped at the ladder Hardy had been using that morning. He clamped the box under one arm and slowly started up. He could look into the little lighted room next to Mam's where Babe was folding down the spread. He climbed on past and laid the box on the roof. He could feel the little tremors of the ladder as Idalee followed rung by rung.

"Your folks will skin you," he said, when they were sitting with their hands flat on the still-warm shingles. She lifted a Roman candle. "And me too. For letting you." He found another Roman candle for himself and lit them both. They pointed the long tubes toward the stars. Little cannonballs of light shot out.

"Oh," she breathed at each color. "Oh, Salty. Look."

They shot off two Whirling Dervishes that spun with golden sparks. Then two smoke bombs on the tin of the gutter. He said, "I'm going to save the rest. Till Hardy comes."

They lay back and looked at the sky. Salty's toes tingled at the thought of the roof edge, the drop into space. He wondered if, out there in the starry sky, the dark cloud of hard times was building up, the way Rose Ann had dreamed.

After a while she asked the sky, "Salty, you like me?"

He braced softly against the question. Who could like anyone going on ten? "I don't know nothing about you."

"Do you have to know somebody?"

"Yes," he said, thinking of Tom and the years they had missed.

"But I like you already," she said. "Just because I want to."

He didn't know how that could work. But he had seen how Jo had loved Micah even before he was born, for whatever he was going to be.

"Could you try?" she asked.

"How?"

"You just start. Could you?"

He slowly propped on his elbows and nodded. But he was thinking of Tom and all the things that were possible, even now. Even yet.

A light went on at the Eversoles.

"Oh, jeeters," Idalee said. "That's my room."

She disappeared down the ladder. He saw the white blur as she shot across the street and in at the front door. She would catch it, he guessed. He hoped what they had done was worth the consequences, and that her daddy didn't have a new hairbrush.

He hadn't let her do a sparkle stick. He sat with his arms

wrapped around his shins, wishing he had, until the light went off in her room.

He looked around. He guessed he would be up there, plenty of times, fixing the roof.

He took his punk stick from between his knees and touched it to a Sphinx. A flame rose, as green as love, and burst into sparks, snow, goose down, tears — he wasn't sure which. But it was for everything that was his, out there.

Quickly he groped in the box and put his punk to a sparkle stick. The gray-coated wire flickered and faded, unable to catch. Then sparkles burst from the grayness, flying, hot against his skin. He stood up, so Idalee could see from her window, and conducted a band of chimneys. He made a great charmed circle over the Buckley Arms, and wrote his name in light.